WATER UNDER THE BRIDGE: A PSYCHOLOGICAL THRILLER

THE WATER TRILOGY | BOOK ONE

BRITNEY KING

WWW.BRITNEYKING.COM

COPYRIGHT

Hot Banana Press

Cover Design by Britney King LLC

Cover Image by Grant Reid Photography

Copy Editing by Librum Artis Editorial Services &

RMJ Manuscript Services

Proofread by Proofreading by the Page

First Edition: 2016

ISBN: 978-0-9966497-2-8 (Paperback)

ISBN: 978-0-9966497-4-2 (All E-Books)

britneyking.com

For the Lovers—
for there are few things as easy or as hard as loving.

WATER UNDER THE BRIDGE

BRITNEY KING

PREFACE

There's a girl long dead who rests down by the water's edge.
Her final words were, "No. Don't. Please. I'm sorr—."
She never did get the second half of her apology out.
I made sure she never will.
Some things are best left unsaid, I think.
In the end, it didn't matter.
I knew she was sorry.
And she knew it too.

There's a girl who rests down by the water's edge.
She was beautiful, but you and the water
washed it all away.
You think I don't know what you've done,
but I do.
I know that you visit on occasion,
and I know other things too.

CHAPTER ONE

JUDE

AFTER

Your face crumbles as the judge hands down our sentence. I am fascinated by the way your expression changes, as slowly, recognition takes over that unlike the rest of your affairs, this one isn't going to be a one-and-done deal. Turns out, lucky us, the great State of Texas is having a go at a pilot program designed to drop the state's divorce rate.

But you aren't feeling very lucky. Not at all. I can tell by the way you pinch the bridge of your nose. You've always hated not getting your way. It doesn't matter anyway. I want to tell you—whatever political agenda bullshit this latest program entails—I can assure you and the rest of Texas, it won't save us. Even if I were the kind of man who believed in miracles, you and me, we'd need a miracle plus a Hail Mary. You've said it yourself, where we are concerned, there is no hope. And this is why you plead.

"Excuse me, your Honor—," you start, and you pause for effect, always the performer. "This really isn't necessary," you profess and then you swallow, and I like it when you're unsure. You go on. "My hus—Jude and I—," you tell him, and you look over at me, and my god, Kate, you've always done indifference so well. "I think we can both agree we're ready to get on with our lives."

You refer to me as your husband—or almost, anyway—and for a moment, I recall what it felt like before your words were laced with poison, back when there was nothing but hope.

I listen to you say your piece, and this time is no different than all the times before, only this time, we have witnesses, and you know how I've always hated that. You must know this because you sink back in your chair, proud.

Your pride doesn't last long because when the judge lists out the terms of our captivity, you glare at your attorney, willing her to save you, but she won't—she can't. You almost choke when he orders six months of marriage counseling, which includes weekly appointments. Your hand flies to your throat, and I remember what that's like, holding you in place, having it all in the palm of my hand. I'd give anything—maybe even your life—to know what that feels like again.

The good news here is the judge and I seem to be on the same page as he informs the two of us that a therapist of our choosing must sign off before the court will grant our divorce. You hold your breath as he speaks, and I remember what that felt like too.

I try, for you, though… I do. I wait for him to finish, and then I tell him that you're right, we've made our decision, and as I speak, you sulk, but isn't this what you've always wanted, to be right? It's hard to look at you, sulking or other-wise, and it never used to be this way.

You're tanner than the last time I saw you. But then, I guess time away did you good. You said you needed your space, and I let you have it. But you have to know, Kate, it was hard not to follow. Maybe I should have. But it was all the same to you—you made up your mind, and your decision settled mine.

Nevertheless, if there is such a thing as a clean break for you and me, it isn't looking good, and it certainly won't be handed down today. This judge does not cease his interminable vendetta against your freedom. He does not relent. You aren't happy, and I can't recall the last time you were, even though I try. It'll come to me, the memory of you, but this courtroom is too stuffy, and you know how I've always hated an audience.

The judge looks away, and you look on, defeated; it's clear, even if you refuse to let it show. As he jots something down, you bite your lip, a tell—you still believe there's hope. But I know better. When he looks up, holding a pen and our future in his hands, you tell him you'd be better off dead, and he looks surprised, as though he's missed something. He has. A lot of somethings. He asks if there's a history of violence. No, you tell him, it was just an expression. Although a part of me wonders if you're right about that too. Maybe there's truth in what you say. Maybe you would be better off dead, and I can't help but wonder if I have it in me.

You text, and there's something about seeing your name light up my phone that still gets me even after all this time. You're all business with your words, and I remember how much I've always liked this side of you. You write that our first therapy session is on Tuesday, and it's so like you to take control, so like you to try and set the pace. But you are mistaken, Kate. Our first therapy session is Monday, and you seem to forget that I'm always one step ahead. You cease with the texting and ring me instead because you like to be the one calling the shots. You're ready to pounce when I offer formalities I don't mean—meanwhile, I'm just happy to hear your voice. You sound exasperated, and I wish I could see your face. No one tells you how much you can miss a person's face. You rattle off instructions, but we don't talk about things, not really, and I wonder when we stopped talking.

We're talking now, that's what you'd say. But I won't—because no one's really saying anything. Nothing worth saying, anyway. Eventually, after I've refused to take the bait because I won't give you my anger as freely as you give yours, you relent, and you agree to the Monday appointment. You'd never admit it, but you like it when I put you in your place. Better to get it over with, you tell me with an edge. The sooner to see you, my dear, I think. But I don't say this. I give you what you want. I always have.

You sit cross-legged with your hands folded neatly in your lap, and I hate how pretty you look. Your hair is up, neat and orderly, different, and I study that spot on your neck, the one I know so well. It's your weak spot, and given the chance, I'd dive right in. But we're here, not there, in more ways than one, and I hate that this middle-aged doctor is checking you out. I don't know why you had to wear such a low-cut top, and I recognize the look he gives you. He has a weakness too. But he thinks he's the one in charge here—I can tell by the way he wears it via the chip on his shoulder—when, in reality, he lacks a real MD behind his name. He'd better watch himself. I'll kill him if I have to. He isn't old, the way I'd imagined, and I silently curse myself for not doing more research on something so important.

"Dr. C." That's how he introduces himself, and it's clear

he's the kind of fellow who believes in make-believe. What a joke this is—what a joke he is. We would laugh about this, you and I, if things were different. If now were before. But it isn't, and no one's laughing.

"So...why don't you tell me where things went wrong...?" he urges, and I want to hate him, and I almost do, but I admire his directness. I, too, am eager to get to the point.

You shrug, and then I do the same because I'm well-versed in the art of mirroring, but mostly because I want to know your answer. I'm glad he starts here because he doesn't know us, Kate, this fake doctor. He doesn't know that other doctors (both real and fake) have told us we're not capable of love. But we were capable, you and I. We were. We weren't make-believe like this guy. We didn't pretend we were something we weren't until we did—and that is the real reason we're here, but I don't say this. I let you lead the way.

"Is there really any way to know, Doc—" you start and then you stop. You don't call him 'doctor,' but you let him think he's in charge, and I like that you're on to him, too. You know his ability to ask a good question doesn't make him a real doctor, and this is a good start. Already, we're getting somewhere, you and I, and I'm starting to feel something that looks a lot like hope.

You are right, I tell him. There's really no way of knowing where things went bad, no way to pinpoint exactly who's at fault, and yet here we are, sitting in these chairs, talking to him instead of each other, both wanting nothing more than to be anywhere else, getting on with our lives.

You nod, and we're on the same page again, and all of a sudden the world seems less bleak.

He asks how we met, and you crinkle your nose.

"Does it really matter?" I ask. "It's over," I say. "Isn't it best to let it be?" I add for good measure, showing that I, too, can ask good questions. You sit up a little straighter, but you drop your guard.

"Perhaps," he says, even though he and I both know he doesn't mean it. *Perhaps*. Give me a break. He doesn't know how much I hate that word, but you do, and I see the corners of your lips turn upward as he says it. It doesn't matter, though. He isn't fooling me with his half-hearted response. 'Dr. C' is a man used to being right. He likes control, he likes being in charge, he gets off on toying with people's emotions, and perhaps I could show him the error of his ways.

"And yet—," he adds, as though he's exasperated when he hardly knows what it means to lift a finger, "I want to go back to where it began." He speaks to me as he looks at you, and I can't blame him. They say living well is the best form of revenge. They are right, and in this case, it's pretty apparent —I am bad at revenge.

"I think it would be a good idea for the two of you to tell each other the story of your coming together—in writing," he says, looking from you to me and back, and I can't be mad at him for staring at your tits when he has such good ideas. "I find writing helps clients come to terms with the dissolution of their marriage in a way that merely talking doesn't…" he continues, pausing for added effect, and you cross your arms. "Writing can be reflective. I find it helps my clients to move on, and more importantly, it lends to healthier relationships in the future."

"I don't write," you tell him, as you shift in your seat—you little liar, you. You write all the time.

"You wrote the text you sent me about this very appointment," I say because he needs to know those tits he's staring at are *my* tits and that we still talk. You give me that look, the one I know so well, and perhaps you are onto me.

"Just give it a try," the fake doctor insists, adjusting his glasses on his nose, and I'd pay money to prove they aren't even prescription. "Trust me," he says, and I don't. I hope you don't either. "It'll save the two of you time talking to me," he adds. It's a small offer of condolence, and thankfully, he says something I like. Only this guy doesn't know you like I do. He may have me convinced, but he hasn't convinced you, and you are not soothed. I can tell by the way you check your phone every two and a half seconds. You're distracted, and you don't trust him. You don't want to talk to him, and I hate that phone for getting more of you than you give to us.

"What happens if I just don't come back?" you ask, and this isn't a threat—you genuinely want to know. You, always the stubborn one, always the one to test the limits, until suddenly, you just don't.

"Well—" he says, and I can tell you've tested him. He's intrigued by your defiance, and I will squash him if he gets any ideas...just like I will squash that phone of yours if you don't stop staring at it. "It's mandatory if you want to wrap up your divorce," he tells you, and I like the direction he's going. I like that he plays hardball, so I don't have to. "Furthermore, you'd be violating a court order, and of course, that's not something I'd advise."

You look over at me, and I smile, and you are so clever. You're not the kind of girl who enjoys being backed against the wall—until you are, and that's exactly what I'm imagining doing right now. I think he is too, and perhaps I'll let it slide, but only because I can tell by your expression you understand he's forcing you to come back here, back to me.

"Fine," you say, and it's too bad you're not a mind reader.

"I'll give it a try," you tell him, and you sigh. You check your phone again, and this is a new one, but then, you've always surprised me with your intelligence. You look up, only this time not at me, and I get that familiar pain in my chest I know all too well. "Now, can I go?" you ask, raising your brow, and you're ready to pounce if the answer that comes isn't the one you want.

"Yes," he says, and you stand. You're about to bolt when he stops you with the flick of a wrist, and I remember when I could do that. "That is—if you agree, Jude. I need a commitment here that you'll both come prepared with something in hand by our next appointment," he adds, and there's authority in his voice when he speaks. You wait, and you listen, and this isn't the girl I know. He's looking at me now as though he and I are on the same team. We aren't, and he can't know how much you both love and hate authority, and maybe this is the answer to his question about where it all went wrong.

"Sure," I tell him, offering my best smile. "I'll come up with something for you, Doc," I offer as though I'm his star student, when in fact, I'm full of shit. But he buys it, and you are antsy because you know I've won. "I'll write you a whole book, if that's what it takes," I add for good measure. He smiles. "I'll call it Water Under the Bridge," I say, fucking with you. You shake your head at me. Then you roll your eyes and start for the door. I'm pretty sure you know he's checking out your ass, and he'd better watch himself. There was a time when this wouldn't have bothered me, a time when I believed in you... when I believed in us.

Now is not that time.

~

CHAPTER TWO

LYDIA

BEFORE
Somewhere, South America

It's 8:07 A.M. on a Wednesday when I see you, a day I'm sure is nondescript to the rest of the world, but not for us. You don't know it yet, but you're my future. I, on the other hand, sense it immediately.

You, with your crisp white shirt and too-clean khaki shorts, you look like a tourist. But there's something in the way you hold yourself, and I can tell you're the kind of person who couldn't care less. Personally, I like the way you blend. You don't belong here. You know it, and I know it—but I am here and so are you. You kick a bit of sand, dig your foot in, and I can tell you're the kind of guy who's in it for the long haul. You seem surprised by the lack of effort it takes to make the sand and the earth move, and you remove your ball cap and scratch your head. Your hair is the color of coal, and the way it sits atop your head, it's as though it has been tousled just for me. I watch you take a few steps toward me, toward our future, and I thank someone somewhere for delivering to me exactly the kind of birthday gift I've been waiting for all my life.

You haven't seen me looking at you. Not yet. But you will. I want to make things easy for us, always. So I make my move. We pass each other, but you do not look up, you do not make eye contact, and I love that you're secure enough in yourself that you don't bother with pleasantries even though you sense the other person expects it.

I'm imaging our first conversation, and later, our wedding, when you plop down in the sand and make a home for us. You pull a pair of sunglasses from your pocket and slide them on. They're designer shades. It's cloudy, and already, you surprise me.

You watch a little girl out in the surf, bobbing and bouncing, thrilled more and more as each wave comes crashing into her, and she looks so familiar that, for a moment, I wonder whether I'm really seeing her at all. But you make her real. I want to go to her—in my daydream, we scoop her up and make her ours. I don't go to her, though, and I don't scoop her up because I know these things have to happen organically. Her mother calls to her, and I find it funny how people sense things. Her name is Sarah, and you smile because you sense things, too.

You're so close and yet so far away. Even still, it's almost impossible to believe my good fortune. You've checked into the bungalow next door. I have five days with you according to the landlord, an old man with just about three teeth left in his head. You have come to me—despite the shenanigans of the past year, I've woken up here next to you, even if not exactly. It's my thirty-fourth birthday, and you have arrived in paradise where the sun shines and the water beckons, and we are free.

You haven't spoken to me yet—although today is the day —the day we will meet officially. You'll suggest coffee, I'll agree, and I will tell you all the stories of my life. I won't lead with the fact that I've gotten away, free and clear, with kidnapping and murder and a whole plethora of charges— even though you seem like the kind of guy who might be impressed by such things. I won't tell you about the voices. I won't have to because the voices have stopped.

Also, because you don't need to know everything. Not yet. We have time. You and I... we have forever. In the meantime, I'll tell you about leaving the States, because you're American, I can tell from the start. You'll listen intently as I share the details of how I've set myself up here, in this tiny little touristy coastal village deep in South America, where the people are kind, and for the most part, keep to themselves. We will always have this place in common, and I like that idea. We are our own compasses. We're different and yet already we like the same places, the same things. It's all very nice, as my father used to say. You will agree when I say we shouldn't give away our location, not to family, not to friends, not to anyone, because you know what else my father always said? Build it and they will come. He was right, and you have come, and you are the kind of person who knows the best secrets are those that are kept.

WE DIDN'T MEET TODAY. NOT OFFICIALLY. INSTEAD, YOU WILL now officially go down in my book as the guy who ruined my birthday. Which is too bad, really. We're supposed to be together, we were supposed to meet via a staged run-in. I had it all planned. Our chance encounter would lead to a long walk on the beach and from there, to the rest of our lives. But you don't leave your bungalow for the rest of the day, and so there is no run in. I knock, but you don't answer, and I'm not sure where you could've possibly gone. This town is small, and you are a mystery. I like this about you, but I hate it too. I grill the landlord, and I study the lines around his eyes as he says you've come alone. They disappear when he tells me he thinks you mentioned meeting a friend, and I don't like the way he uses this word friend. It's clear—he knows as well as I do that most people don't travel to exotic locales to meet friends of the same sex, and I hope I am wrong about this, about you. The next morning, the landlord tells me you've checked out. But how can it be that you are gone? How can we be over when we've only just begun? This is how I know it's time to make a change.

I have to find you.

You need to know the only friend you need is me.

~

CHAPTER THREE

JUDE

Nothing is simple with you, and I like things simple, clean. But this is ok, it has to be. Nothing is perfect right out of the gate, and we will get there. All things are fixable, except a few—one of those being death. The short end of it... the simple version is that you are a killer, and I've been hired to turn you in—to bring you to justice. I won't tell you this, at least not at first, but that's why I came. It isn't, however, why I stay.

I stay for you. For us. Only, you were interested, and I got too close, and now I'll have to move to 'Plan B' and you don't know this about me yet—but you will—I'm not a 'Plan B' kind of guy. I like to get it right the first time. Even more so where you are concerned.

You aren't like most girls. You weren't easy to find, and I've been looking for one version or another of you for as long as I can remember. You don't splash the details of your life all over the internet, and you aren't on social media, cataloging your every move for strangers you call friends. You don't post staged pictures of what you're having for dinner, and you don't take pictures of your food to show how healthy you are, and I like this. I'll learn your desires, slowly, the way it's meant to be.

You don't need everyone to know where you are, what you're doing, to show how great your life is. You don't seek approval by shouting into the ether, into what I call the great want-to-be-known. You're not like the masses—most people lay it all out there at the curb like garbage on trash day, and I'll tell you what that does—it makes the whole neighborhood stink. It's okay, for now, that I'm not sure if this is because you can't let people know—or because you're just the kind of girl I like—but I'm optimistic. I choose to go with the latter.

You like intimacy, you like really knowing people. You're the kind of girl who prefers long conversations deep into the night or in the small moments before the sun rises ... moments hazy and real. This makes you the kind of girl I can get behind. In every sense.

This morning, I heard you wake and rise from your slumber because I listen for the sounds of you. I want to know you, I want to know everything. This is how I know you're up with the sun, and we were made for each other. I listen as you go into the bathroom and do your business, and I hope to God you're the kind of girl who washes her hands afterward. I listen to the water run as you turn it on full force, and I am in luck, it seems you are. But you take forever in there, and I'm not sure exactly what you could be doing that lasts so long. But then you are beautiful, and everyone knows that beauty takes time.

Eventually, I hear your voice, and it's perfect. I wonder who you're talking to, and I intend to find out. I say a silent thank you that these so-called walls are paper thin.

"Thank you, Daddy," you say, and you and I, we know gratitude. Still, I know that your father is dead, and you are a dirty girl with daddy issues, you are. "This is the best gift I could possibly receive," you say, but you are wrong.

You have the water running again, and now I can't hear anymore. So I climb out of bed and rush to the bamboo slat I've removed between our bungalows just so I can see you because I can't miss a thing. My eyes hurt from straining, but there you are, and I can breathe now that I have a visual. You're in your panties, lace, with nothing on top, and you are not holding a phone. You move away, and I hate it when you hide from me. You're still talking, and I'm still waiting when suddenly, I can see just a sliver of your silhouette. I wait for more. I could wait forever until you come into full view again. Only, when you finally do, you are crying, and you should only ever know happiness.

"I know, Daddy," you whimper, but you are talking to no one, something in a mirror that doesn't exist and maybe we all have our demons. "You're right, I'm not getting any younger," you cry as you stare into your reflection, into the invisible Daddy version of yourself, and then you sink to your knees. "I know I have no one—I have nothing. You always tell me this... but why today?" you demand, and you stammer, dig your heels in. You are a fighter, I can tell.

"Of course, I want to make you proud," you tell him, and no one, and you sigh. You shouldn't have conversations that wear you down, and someday, I will tell you this. For now, I just listen. "You know I do," you go on, and this is getting uglier than I imagined. But then again, how can I be anything other than turned on at the sight of you at the altar, bowing to your demons, begging for mercy?

"I met someone today, Daddy," you confess. "He's staying next door... And... maybe—" you tell your make-believe father, and maybe make-believe isn't so bad after all because my best and worst fears are confirmed in your confession. You know there's something between us, and now I know for sure. You're drawn to me too. This is good, and this is very, very bad, and only you and I know how that can be.

"I get it," you say, "you want me to start a family. You think I need to settle down—but you've said it yourself, Daddy—perhaps—I'm just not that kind of girl."

I will make you that kind of girl. I will make you a woman, a woman who isn't confused about what she wants, who doesn't need anyone else deciding for her. You could be that woman—I can see it now.

"Look at me, Daddy," you seethe. You wring your hands, and you pace, coming in and out of view. "You always tell me that I have no one—that I'll die just like you—on an empty mattress on the floor. And you're right—no one will care... because there is no one. And, yes, I realize that if I keep doing what I'm doing, you are right, nothing will change. Daddy, I know. This is no way to live," you say, and you're sobbing now, and you are mistaken. I will care.

"Yes, Daddy," you repeat again as you attempt to contain your tears. "I need someone who will punish me, and then you will be happy and then you will go."

You pause and inhale. You don't let it out, and I wonder where all the pent up stuff goes, and I think I have an idea. "Ok, fine," you tell your reflection. "This time, I will listen. I promise," you tell your imaginary father. You wipe your eyes, and my god, those panties hug your ass in a way that makes me jealous, and I have to know about this punishment you speak of. You are naughtier than I thought, and I think I could love a risk-taker like you. I'm so lost in my own desires for a moment that I almost miss it when you begin to slip further.

"No, you're not dead," you scream into the mirror, and now you are angry, and this is good that I get to see another side of you. I want to know them all. "YOU'RE HERE. YOU'RE HERE," you scream until, eventually, you sink to the ground. You are sobbing now, and I am captivated by your performance—you're either crazy, or you have mad talent, and I am excited to think it's a little of both.

You do want a family. I heard you say it, and this is why I can't turn you in even if it's an assignment.

You want someone to share your life with and guess what? I'm on the market.

You just have to stop running, Lydia.

You have to come home to me.

WHEN YOU GO OUT, I GO IN AND TODAY IS YOUR BIRTHDAY, and I am not happy with what I find. Your place is a pigsty, Lyd. A fucking mess. I can't be with a girl who lives like this, and maybe the imaginary father you speak to in the mirror is right—maybe you can't manage yourself.

This is made obvious by the fact that I can so easily break and enter your bungalow, and by the fact that I can do what I want with that which is yours. You don't lock your laptop, it isn't password protected, and why do you have to make things so easy when clearly you have so much to hide? Not that I'm complaining, Kate. Wait. Can I call you Kate now? Tell me, is it too early? Or shall I wait a day or two?

You have plans, and you don't hide them well, and according to your calendar, you're at the hair salon becoming a brunette, and everyone knows blondes have more fun. You are changing, and you are running again, and this is good—except that it isn't—not when your email tells me what you have in the works. You shouldn't have your passwords stored in your notes, and my god, we have a lot of work to do. And by work, I'm not referring to the plastic surgery you have scheduled, and I understand the need to be something different than that which you are—but you don't need work, Kate—you don't.

Also, you talk to yourself. I hear you at all hours, and when do you sleep? I enjoy my shut-eye, and it's no wonder your life is such a mess.

You've booked a flight to Brazil, but I can't follow you there. I have assignments and deadlines, and I would follow you to the ends of this earth if we were together, but we're not. Yet.

You think changing your hair and your face will help you fit in, but guess what, Kate? You are wrong about that too— because wherever you go, there you are.

YOUR BROWSER HISTORY TELLS ME YOU'VE SCOURED THE internet looking for the best diet around and why would you ever want to lose those curves? Furthermore, why can't you just be a respectable adult and delete your history so I don't have to read such bullshit and ruin my whole day?

You set a calendar appointment with yourself to lose twenty pounds. I know this because I've set up your cloud on my phone and the fact that it's so easy to spy on you, to know everything there is to know about you, signifies everything that is wrong with our generation. Technology is ruining us, and maybe there is such a thing as too much too soon.

IT'S HARD TO BE ANGRY WITH YOU ABOUT BRAZIL, ABOUT THE surgery, and the weight loss when I tap into your writing. It's hard to be mad at technology when I stop and think about it. I should be grateful that it's so easy to take a tiny hard drive and download the contents of your life. I'm learning so much about you, Kate. Things like how you were in love once. His name was James, and you were seventeen and your writing assures me that he was perfect —but no one is. He lived down the street, and you loved him before you 'snapped' (your words), and maybe this is okay because you are different now, and our love will be too.

They locked you away, and now I'm starting to get it. Now, I understand why you're such a mess. I read your diagnosis, and everything is laid out so neatly, now—thanks to this little black box. You don't feel things the way other people do, and the pieces that make you up are beginning to fit together in my mind. You're a puzzle, Kate, and I haven't told you how much I like your new name, but someday, I plan to.

Anyway, your father thought you and this guy were getting too close, so he moved you across town. But you're a clever girl, and you feel things deeply. You hang on when the going gets tough. Of course, a little distance wouldn't change that, and so you continued seeing him even if it wasn't as often as before, and there's something about your defiance that turns me on.

This kid, James, had plans to go away to art school in Colorado that fall, and you'd promised to go with him, and I love that you're willing to follow your heart.

But you're sensitive and naïve, Kate, and James didn't love you the way you loved him. I'm sorry to ruin the story for you. I know this because you had no plans for yourself— unless you count working your ass off to put him through school, banking on the fact that dear ol' James had the talent and the wherewithal to make something of himself.

Not to spoil the ending for you—but most artists don't. You thought it was okay that things would be hard in the beginning because you'd have each other. But what you don't understand about love, Kate, is that the beginning is supposed to be the best part.

Still, it's sweet the way you write about that summer—the summer after graduation, about how you spent every waking moment together and the way you tell it—it's almost as good as a goddamned Nicolas Sparks novel. Not that I've ever read one—but I'd be willing to bet money that you have.

But you surprise me, too, by how you can go from Sparks to Stephen King in the matter of a few paragraphs when you write about your mother, and my god, after reading this, I'm impressed you seem as normal as you do.

You had big dreams, you did. Albeit a little misguided. You keep secrets, and your mother is weak, and you're wrong —it was your father who was the sick one.

They didn't care that you didn't plan to go to college. And it's wrong the way your father convinced you it was best you stick close to home to help with your mother. She was sick in the way that people get when they can't leave the house. She rarely made you dinner and almost never did things normal mothers do, and the more I read, the more I realize we are the same, you and I.

There were weeks she didn't leave the confines of her bedroom, and this made you anxious because no one aside from your father was allowed to enter, and you don't say it in words, but you were practically an orphan, like one of those Russian babies forced to fend for themselves.

And not even just for yourself. It went further than that. You were like fucking Cinderella. You cooked for her, you took her food and left it by the door. You'd knock once, knowing she couldn't—or wouldn't answer—and your father always told you what a waste she was, but he left out the part where it was his fault. Most of the time, you'd scrape her food and your hard work down the disposal all the while you wondered how long someone could survive on a mixture of coffee and vodka and cigarettes, and I can attest that given my own mother's disappearance, it isn't forever.

You didn't know your mother, not the way I knew mine. She rarely spoke to you, but what could she possibly have had to say, living that way? Saying as much probably wouldn't make you feel better, and someday, I will tell you that it's okay—that it's hard to really know a person anyway.

You have ambition, Kate and not fake aspirations like that guy you loved, either. You were determined to get out. So you stowed away cash you earned in tips, and this is what set the two of you apart. You were willing to work for what you wanted. But your mistake was handing over the money you earned from waitressing to your father. You were young and naïve—but you weren't dumb—and so you saved a portion of your tips, hidden away. I appreciate your cleverness even if he didn't.

And I know he didn't because, when he found your stash, it set off a whole chain of events that made you the person you are today, and so maybe it's okay. If not, it will be, just give me time. I'll make it that way.

Speaking of time, it was just a mere five days before you and James were set to depart that things went south, and fast. You returned home excited, which was only elevated by the fact you found your mother sitting on the couch waiting for your return, the way a normal mother might, only you hadn't seen yours in eighteen days. Freedom was within reach, and your mother was no longer locked away, and you felt hope for the first time in a long time. That is until your father called from the kitchen. You will never forget the way your heart swelled before you heard his voice, and the more I read, the more mine breaks for you.

It breaks at the part where your mother finally speaks to you, and when she does, it's only to tell you that your room has bad things in it. But her heart doesn't break because it doesn't know love like mine. There's bad energy in there, she tells you, and I'm not sure if you know it, but she's the bad energy, and it's your family who is crazy, not you.

Your father finds you in the living room. He finds you everywhere. He's drying his hands when he tells you he ran into James's mother in the grocery store, and you sink to your knees. You pray that the floor will swallow you up, but it won't because it's not quicksand you walk on in that house —it's eggshells. He informs you that your mother found the money—but I'd be willing to bet it was him even though it doesn't really matter because the outcome is the same. He doesn't tell you they've destroyed your bedroom, your hopes, your dream. You just know.

You don't go down easy, though—not without a fight. You know what comes next, and you won't let him lock you in that room, not this time, not again. You won't become a younger version of your mother, you tell him. But then, that's what all girls say.

You thought you could run, but this was before you got good at it.

You thought they couldn't stop you. But you were wrong. They could, and they did. And they drove you to the brink in the process. They knew what to say to put you where they wanted you to be. In your room, in your place. You grabbed carpet by the fistful before you moved to the hair on your head—anything— you said to avoid being punished—to avoid being locked in that room.

The thing is, your father understood what you didn't, Kate. He understood the long game. He'd been playing it longer.

He told the police, and then the doctors, that you attacked him, and they bought into his lies, but not me. You didn't have it in you—not then.

Unfortunately, no one knew this. Maybe they should've

read your writing, but they didn't, and so they locked you away for ten weeks. And, Kate—that boy you loved... all he did was send a note thanking you for the money your father sent. Money that was yours and all he had to say for himself was that he was sorry you were sick. But, like me, you're a real romantic, one of the few left. This is why you wrote to him every day, often twice a day, bearing your heart, bleeding on the page.

All those letters you sent? They were a monument to your love, but he only ever returned one. He wrote that he missed you and that he was doing well. As a token, he offered a small drawing—of a mountain. It must have meant something to you because you've kept it, even after all this time. It's crap if you ask me. He promised he'd take you there, to see this mountain. But unlike me, he isn't the kind of guy who makes good on his promises. It's hard to blame him, though, given that three weeks after that final letter was sent, you received the news that he was dead.

CHAPTER FOUR

KATE

I t's probably best we didn't meet, not yet. Sometimes people have to prepare themselves for a person, a thing, a life. If we'd had a proper introduction—if you'd asked my name, I'm not sure what I would have told you. My life exists inside the hat of a magician. You could pull a dozen names out, and it wouldn't matter, it's likely any one of them would be right for the moment.

I do my best to look at the bright side even though we weren't properly introduced. Maybe there are no absolutes in life, and maybe you will think it's okay that I can be so many people all wrapped into one. Maybe, you won't think I'm crazy. It isn't as bad as having multiple personalities, but then again, maybe that diagnosis wouldn't be so far from the truth.

If we were to meet today, I would tell you my name is Callie Jones. But that would mostly be a lie. Callie is just another alias in a string of many. By birth, I am Lydia Hartman, a murderer on the run. But that girl is long gone, and she took the name with her. I don't presume to know you well, but I think you would like Callie. I have grown quite fond of her.

It's strange to think of you this way, in the abstract, when you are so real. It feels strange to ponder what you might like and to consider whether or not I have it in me to shape myself into that person. And right now, I'm not so sure, although I want to be. You have a hold on me, the kind that won't let go. It started when I first laid eyes on you and ends with you running through my mind with abandon. You take up space, make it yours. You are a squatter—one I can't get rid of.

But crazy or not, I know what's real and what isn't—and you are not squatting here today, which is too bad because I know you would love this pastel blue sky of summer. I stare at it and think about you reveling in the sound of the waves crashing into one another, in the vastness of the sea. It's breathtaking to know the ocean, to understand that it can swallow you whole and spit you out before you even know what hit you. Being here on this beach, in this moment, it is everything words cannot capture. But then I realize—I don't even know if you care about words—or the sky—or me, and I wonder if I really know anything at all.

Nevertheless, it's nice to be curious, and I do know at least one thing. It's hard to love one person and be with another, and I wonder if you know this, too. The truth of the matter is, I have to find a husband, and it's sad to think that person may not be you. I realize now, sitting here on this beach, in order to find out, Callie Jones has to evolve, like the shedding of skin, the way a caterpillar becomes a butterfly. I can't be Callie and get what I want.

I have to become someone else. Someone new, more desirable, more compatible with the life I want. Kate is someone I think you will like. Kate is the kind of girl you need—whereas Callie was *apparently* the kind who didn't deserve a proper introduction, the kind of girl you run from. Not to worry, though. Kate will be the kind of girl you chase.

I THOUGHT IT MIGHT INTEREST YOU TO KNOW THAT I SENT Callie out with a bang. I am becoming Kate—someone steady, for you—and after all, becoming someone new isn't free. To be comfortable in my new life, I had to make a few bucks and Robin Hood-style seemed a good way to go about it. Take from the rich and give to the poor—socialism at its finest—and I wonder about your politics. I bet you're proud. I bet you'd never accept a handout or a leg up. I bet you're blue blood through and through. I bet you're the kind of man who understands the value of a dollar.

I don't know if you like numbers—but they fascinate me. My whole life has been one mathematical equation I cannot solve. And maybe this is the way it's meant to be—this unknowingness, this perpetual state of limbo—for if we knew the answer, that would solve the question—or if we ran out of them, both questions and answers, we'd be dead.

A problem is only a question you haven't yet found the answer to; at least, that's what my father told me once. It's a sentiment that seems fitting given it has been thirteen days and eight hours since my last kill and this is something I must solve. But then, sometimes things find you and sometimes you find them.

For me, as luck would have it, that *thing* was a woman named Dina and she found me. Dina Polanski, the granddaughter of a Russian immigrant, visiting from The Garden State. Beautiful and fun, for sure—she was also your typical gold digger. Dina was not blue blood through and through, but she was proud. Proud of the fact that she made off with a fair bit of her ex-husband's money after getting 'accidentally' knocked up. You wouldn't like Dina— I know this even without even *really* knowing you—I know because Dina's are hard to like. Even for people like me. *Especially for people like me.* People like Dina are work, and I think you will appreciate knowing that I did, in fact, work hard for every cent I earned off her. I met Dina on her second day here, and just like the others I'd come to know before her, she'd set off in search of a vacation from her normal everyday vacation.

This is why it's fairly easy, in resort towns, to find the Dina Polankskis of the world. You can spot them a mile away, even if you're not looking, and I wasn't because I was too busy thinking about you. But for the sake of a good story, it might be helpful to know that, generally, you'll find them in one of two places: in the daytime, they enjoy lounging by a hotel pool (four-star or above), and after dark, they set up camp in the hotel bar. You'll know one when you see her, no doubt. You'll know because these women are loud and audacious when they're surrounded by familiar company—but if you get them alone and let them sense that you know who and what they are, then suddenly, they become meek, unsure of themselves—and all too eager not to let it show.

True to form, this particular gold digger and I ran into each other at her hotel bar while I was searching for you. Forty-two, with two kids, and two baby daddies to match, both of whom happen to be highly successful. It was easy to know right away what Dina was looking for—a good time, someone to fill the role she wanted, nothing more and nothing less. And suddenly, there it was, or rather there *she* was—the answer to my question. Dina wanted what most women want—she wanted to be needed. She wanted someone to make her feel better about being past her prime. Dina wasn't dumb. She realized that sooner rather than later, the kids would be grown, and the gravy train would inevitably dry up, and all she'd have to show for it are two kids that the help raised and a better understanding of the worthless pond scum she'd allowed herself to become. Dina was looking for the answer to a question, too.

And sure, maybe I was angry about not finding you—maybe I needed to get you off my mind, maybe I needed the money, but the simple fact of the matter was Dina was an easy target. She sought me out—and she sealed the deal when she ordered me a drink even though I hadn't asked. Dina was easy to seduce because I knew what she needed—and I gave it to her. I think you would be proud of my effort.

She'd sworn she'd always wanted to be with a woman, after just an hour together, she confessed she'd even kissed one—way back in college. The way she told the story, her eyes wide, voice low, you would have thought she was special, as though I'd never heard any of it before. Men are easier that way. You don't hand everything over, and I'll never understand why women are incessantly confessing.

But you know what's funny about the whole thing? Dina thought I had money. She thought I was like her, and I let her believe. This is how I won. It's how I always win. When she said she thought I was fun, a nice distraction, I ran with it—I mean, what could a sun-kissed, sand-ridden, love affair possibly hurt? Nothing, she'd whispered as though I were anything but another secret to be kept. *Nothing at all.* She wanted it known that she was traveling to get away from the drama of it all. She was just looking to have fun, she said proudly, after downing her third vodka tonic. Turns out, so was I.

And I gave her fun. You have to know I did. Later, in her oversized walk-in shower, I ate her like she'd never been eaten, and she called my name (Callie) and whispered that maybe she'd never go back to screwing men. *She wouldn't.*

We could have so much fun together, she purred afterward, as she stroked my hair.

Only poor Dina was wrong. It didn't turn out to be very fun for her in the end. Our love affair only lasted three short days and then she was dead.

I have to admit (which isn't the same thing as confessing) that it was nice killing Dina. It took my mind off you, off the future, and put my focus where it belonged—in the present. I would have killed her sooner—she turned out to be a stage ten clinger—had it not taken me that long to get the bank account info I needed in order to make the transfer. Sixty-five thousand dollars in total—half of which I transferred into an American bank account, and the other half, into another. Within a day or two, I transferred the sum of both to another. *Always keep moving.*

I want you to know my MO because it's important you know upfront that I am a rule follower. And I am ruled by my intuition. I feel things. I know who's worth killing. I understand the value of things. I have a certain way I work, and I never take everything. *Ever.* Three-fourths at most. And I never leave money sitting in one spot for long.

I hope you won't think ill of me for saying so, but I won't say I feel bad about the whole thing. Dina Polanski was a mediocre lover at best, and the only thing worse than medi-ocre sex is mediocre sex with a drunk. In that sense, she drank herself to death. That's what the kids who consider the nannies their mothers will think, anyway. It's almost less sad this way, you know? I saved Dina from herself. I saved her from further embarrassment. The men she screwed (literally) will toast unknowingly to this fact, and this is how I know I did a good thing. I know the value of a dollar as well as you do, and I will tell you, I earned that money every bit as much as Dina did. I was just smarter in the way I went about getting it.

These men will thank me. I consider myself an unsung

hero. They'll be delighted to finally be off the hook—thrilled to have one less needy gold digger causing them headaches. Good riddance, they'll say. And later, years down the road, their spoiled children will lament to their therapists how sad it is that their mother drank herself to death. But what they *won't* know is the kind of hell I saved them from. They'll never understand the lesser of two evils, and I wish someone had done me this service. Instead, this will be their crutch, having a dead mother. They'll use it for all kinds of things— for gaining sympathy with teachers, for getting laid—but mostly, as a way of explaining why they never lived up to their full potential. But I guess one has to choose their battles.

Dina never lived up to her potential either. I did her a favor, too. She was as easy to kill as she was to seduce, and this world wasn't meant for easy people. You and I, we understand the concept of survival of the fittest while people like Dina are clueless. She was weak and shallow, and she didn't know love. She used me to make her feel wanted, and I returned the favor by crushing sleeping pills and adding them to her third glass of red. Dina should have known better. She should have known the third time would be the charm. *Three strikes you're out.* Life has rules.

But no, she was hell-bent on learning the hard way, via the firm hotel pillow I used to cover her face as she slept— right after we'd made love—right after she'd called it the best sex of her life. How lucky for her to go out like that, and I bet you like your pillows soft.

Thankfully, only me and Dina—and now you—will ever know the whole truth—that she didn't go away to kill herself, the way an old dog runs away to die.

But then, honestly, how well can we ever really know what goes on inside a person? Just like those old dogs, washed-up Dina did those she loved a favor when she met me. She may not have known love, but she saved them with it, and this is how I will save you.

You see, I'm learning too. I learned the answer to a question from my time with Dina. I learned that whatever I do in the future, one thing is for sure—I never, ever, want to become her.

CHAPTER FIVE

JUDE

I was all of six when I had my first encounter with a monster. It was a Tuesday, laundry day, and I was home from school sick. That afternoon, I was awoken by my mother's screams, and shortly after I came face to face with evil. Wiping the sleep from my eyes, suddenly, I was alert as I'd ever been. I don't think you register right away the difference in the way a scream can sound, maybe that comes in hindsight because I still remember thinking that it was probably another scorpion. My mother hated scorpions. And Dad refused to let pest control in the house—or anyone else for that matter. But I do know that *something* seemed different, and I thought maybe, this time, she'd gotten stung.

Hoping this wasn't the case, I rounded the corner and headed for the first aid kit my father kept under the bathroom sink. Only when I peered down the hall, I could see it was worse—much worse. I could see my mother scuffling with a man I did not know.

I took a deep breath and crossed the hall into my parent's bedroom, without hesitation, feeling boyhood draining from me with each step. By the time I grabbed my dad's .45, any trace of youth I'd had left was gone completely. I put eight rounds into that man. He lived.

It was no secret in our community that my dad was gone a lot. Criminals pay attention to these things. Joe Luis just so happened to be the first of them to find us. Luis was a drifter who hung around outside of our local gas station, and on more than one occasion, I watched as my mom placed her change in the cup he held. Unfortunately for her, Joe Luis knew a pretty lady when he saw one.

My mother was a Good Samaritan and Good Samaritans are easy targets for violent criminals, and this one deserved to die—only he didn't. Instead, he spent sixteen days in the hospital on the taxpayer's dime (something I learned about later) before he was released back onto the streets where he evaded authorities for six months. In the meantime, he committed two additional violent crimes and was well on his way toward the next when he was picked up during a routine traffic stop.

I don't know what you know of karma, and it's funny how things sometimes work out, but for me, I've always preferred not to leave matters as serious as Joe Luis to silly platitudes like karma.

I prefer to take fate into my own hands—I prefer loading the gun and pulling the trigger—if it means one less man out there like him, one less man not hurting more women like my mother, destroying entire families in the process. Thankfully, my father felt the same way and allowed me another stab (pun intended) at ol' Joe. I think you would have been proud of me had you known me then. Joe understood pain in his final hours, and it was *almost* enough penance for what he did to my mother—but not quite.

Even though I promised my mom that I'd always take care of her, and my father that I'd be a better shot the next time, she was never the same after Joe kicked in our door, putting a hole in it and straight through our lives. It mattered little that my father and I took care of Joe. By that point, the damage had been done. From that day on, everything changed. First, my training took an accelerated path and my once carefree and capable mother became skittish and with-drawn. Eventually, she withdrew into herself so far that it was clear even to me she would never find her way out.

You're probably wondering how a six-year-old knew how to shoot a gun, albeit not well, and that would be thanks to Rudy. My father taught me everything I know about every-thing. He, and in a sense the monsters of this world, molded me into who I am today. I am a killer, Kate. Not so very different from yourself. I make a living delivering justice to those who deserve it. But truth be told, I would do it for free, and justice is best when it's handled swiftly. This is why I left South America when I did. I know you think it's because you weren't important enough to stay—but that's where you are wrong. I left because there are other mothers and little boys out there who shouldn't have to suffer because some low-life thinks he can take what isn't his.

I'VE BEEN THINKING A LOT ABOUT IT, KATE, AND YOU KNOW why most people don't get ahead? It's because they're shit at listening. These days, everyone just wants to be heard—*to be known*—but when everyone is so busy trying to be known—then who's listening?

I'll tell you who. People like me. People behind the scenes who work tirelessly to keep people like them safe. Despite the fact that they mess things up on the daily—despite the fact that they refuse to stop vomiting their entire lives all over the internet.

People these days, they give every single detail away—all

for the sake of being *connected*. Nothing it seems is off limits —from their whereabouts—to their favorite things. It doesn't seem to matter in the least that other people (*their "friends"*) don't actually care about every single trivial aspect of their lives. They keep at it.

But some people *do* care, and those people are criminals, and they are the ones who stand to gain the most.

Idiots like these are what make me work so hard. Because behind every moron wanting to be *connected* is a victim waiting to be taken. Sometimes, these victims are among the most vulnerable in our society, little boys and girls whose parents cared more about their *"friends"* knowing all the details of their lives than they do about them.

This is why the world needs more people like me out there taking out the garbage, doing my best to slow the fall down the rabbit hole our society is quickly falling down. And it's a slippery slope, Kate, let me tell you. Nothing seems all that bad until it happens to *you*. People—they think bad things won't happen to them. But they are morons, trying to be *connected,* and they are wrong.

Criminals happen to everyone; I can tell you from experience, they happen, even to hit men and their families, even before the internet. These days, it's just easier.

On the other hand, I can't be too mad about morons or the internet since it led me to you. It leads me to most people, to tell you the truth. It led me to Amy. She was a tyrant. But she is a story for another day.

You are a tyrant too—but at least you choose well. You choose victims that are far from innocent. But then no one is, not really. You have a method of going about things which I find interesting. In fact, to be blunt, I am captivated. You are forcing me to ask questions I never thought I'd ask.

Still, there's the other matter. I have a job to do, and as Rudy would say—a criminal is a criminal. I've been poring over every last detail, trying to justify my failure to do my job where you are concerned, because you're different, and rarely do I meet women who kill. Women are life-givers, through and through. They don't take lives, they give birth to life, and this makes them innately value life more. This is why it's rare to see a woman kill—it usually only occurs as an outcome of being provoked. Most often, you'll find it's a crime of passion. Those I can appreciate. And, if you ask me, even though I'm only one small cog in the wheel of the justice system, it's almost always deserved. But then, that's easy for me to say because I believe in killing when it's warranted. Not everyone deserves to live, and there is a higher order this world would do better to understand.

Speaking of order, this is why I had to get back to the States. This is why I disappeared the way I did. I had a job more pressing than you. A hit on an arms dealer that couldn't wait. The transaction he had in mind—it couldn't be made. Men like him put innocent people at risk for the sake of making a buck. One bullet straight to the heart of the matter —that's all it took. Order was restored—for the moment, at least. But make no mistake, Kate. There will be others.

I'm sorry for leaving before you and I had our shot. But it's important you see the bigger picture in life, Kate. It's important you understand order. You don't realize it quite yet, but I will help you.

As of four days ago, you have settled back in Austin, Texas. You didn't need work done, and I didn't think it was possible, but you look better than ever. You're skinnier than the last time I saw you, but you didn't lose your curves, and I hope you never do. All I know is you're testing the theory that blondes have more fun, and I want in on your game.

In the meantime, you've rented a funky little apartment in a funky part of town, and I watch. You have come home. This seemed an odd choice, coming home, even for you, out of character—given your crimes and the proximity you've just put yourself to the people who know who and what you are.

Yesterday, I watched as you met someone, a man, who I figured was to be your next victim. Only I was wrong, and I hate being wrong—and look at what you're doing to me. So far, he's still alive, and if you're planning on killing this guy, you haven't made your move yet.

Why I'm not sure... the two of you spent the night together so you certainly had the opportunity, and you should know there's nothing worse than wasted opportunities. It's a bummer, really—I didn't think you were that kind of girl. But what do I know? Well, I'll tell you. Actually, I know a lot. I know that you are playing Russian roulette with your life, and you are lucky to have me watching out for you.

I also know from watching this isn't your typical MO—it isn't like you to drag things out. Usually, you're quick—succinct—which only makes this development all the more perplexing. I hate to consider it, but I do—maybe you like this guy, and this is why I have to get closer. Sure, it's dangerous. Rudy would even go so far as to say stupid—but I need a face-to-face with you. I realize now this is inevitable. I need to talk to you, Kate. I need to understand what makes you tick. Mostly, I need to know why I haven't completed this job.

After all, I've spent weeks studying your crimes, and it didn't take me long to figure out how you work. You stalk your targets well—you seduce them—and you murder them shortly thereafter. Usually, within a day or two. The most I've seen you wait was three. You're good at making your kills appear as though they were suicides, and this makes you different than most serial killers. But then, this much I knew the first time I laid eyes on you. You don't flaunt your kills—you hide them well. You're clever—entertaining to watch, and I wonder if you work as hard as I do. I wonder if you still have love for the game, or if like me, it's wearing on you.

Maybe the money helps—or maybe, for you, it's about winning. Admittedly, at first, I was convinced robbery was your motive. Because that would make sense.

But, now, I realize it's more than that.

And this is the part I'm dying to figure out.

I FOLLOW YOU TO A COFFEE SHOP WHERE YOU MEET ANOTHER man—which should make me angry. But it doesn't. In part, because it isn't the same man as before, which tells me you like variety, and this is good. But also because seeing the two of you together, this is how I guess at what you're doing.

I realize now you're meeting your targets online. A hunch tells me likely on a dating site. This is a development I hadn't expected. You are a beautiful woman. The kind men and women flock to, and so I have to know, why are you sinking this low? I can't stop watching because I have to know how low you're willing to go, Kate. Tell me. No, show me—where exactly *is* rock bottom for you? I hope for your sake this is it, and this is why I have to find out which site.

So I keep watching even though it makes me sick. I'm not used to feeling this way and let me tell you, I deal in some messed up shit. I watch you play cat and mouse. But there are bigger cats than you, Kate. It would do you well to remember that. You're practically a kitten sitting there. I see the way you look as you chat the guy up, all flirty and charming in the way you laugh. You touch his arm as you speak, and you are so good at pretending that, for a moment, even I have a tough time telling whether you're playing him or not. But you have to be because, aside from having shifty eyes—which makes it obvious that he is hiding something (who isn't)—he seems rather plain. Too plain for a girl like you and why are you staying so long? You're leaving the door open, you're inviting him in, and you should have shut the door sooner. You should have walked out that door and into my life because I am not plain, and look at you wasting time. *Women. I swear, I'll never understand what makes them tick.* Luckily for you, part of my job is figuring out what makes people do what they do, and from now on, I intend to make a better effort.

You've dressed up for him too, in a t-shirt dress and fancy sandals. I know when women are trying to make an impression, and Kate, you are trying too hard. But I would be lying if I said you look anything less than stunning—and I must say I'm impressed with your resourcefulness.

Even after all this time, this is the thing that always surprises me about killers—how very, very smart they are.

You, though, *you* take the cake. You're brilliant—even at rock bottom, and I need to know more. I need to be inside your head. I need to see what makes you, you.

Which is why I don't go at all easy on 'shifty eyes' when I finally make his acquaintance. To save myself a few hours of internet research and even more time spent creating fake personas, I decide to take the road less traveled. I follow him into the parking garage where I grab him from behind. People really should be more aware of their surroundings. He isn't your type, Kate. You need a challenge, and you should know that he didn't even put up a fight, and seriously, this is the kind of guy you're into? I hate thinking of you this way, as easy, but I can't help it. It's irritating, and so I let off steam by pressing against his carotid artery. I don't let go until he is close to passing out, and then, because I can relate to the fellow—after all, *it is* hard to resist your charm—I release the choke-hold, and I demand to know how he knows you.

You should also know that the poor bastard told me what I needed to know without the slightest hint of hesitation, which was an excellent sign for me but terrible for you. He sold you out, Kate. What kind of man gives information to an attacker about someone they care about? I'll tell you—the kind who doesn't deserve you, and you have to know this.

And you will, thanks to the fact that cowards in this world are a dime a dozen—and thanks to the information this one so effortlessly offered up, lo and behold, three days from now… you and I have a date.

CHAPTER SIX

KATE

The funny thing about humans—I've learned—is that if there's one thing we excel at, it's seeking love from those who are least likely, or willing, to give it. So, of course, it only makes perfect sense once I've settled back in Austin that I've begun my search for a husband on a very popular, well-known dating app. It is all so simple and who knew finding forever could be so easy? This app lets you find and hook up with random people in your vicinity. Just like that, with the swipe of a finger, *you can* have it all.

Or so I thought. I swipe through profile after profile of boys that claim to be men and the odds aren't looking good, and still, I decide to go on. I decided to no longer be the kind of girl who waits around, and so I go on these dates anyway. You should know, I'm finished standing on the sidelines—I'm ready to play the game. But it doesn't take long to realize that games need rules and so does the mate selection process.

It's not that I'm a stranger to one-night stands—it's just that most of my lovers end up dead. But even I know that's no way to land a husband.

It's just that by the third date in, I hate men—and I hate

husband hunting. This sucks—if I can't even get through a date or two without so much rage, then what are the odds of spending the rest of my life with someone?

I tried to be wrong about the odds of finding and landing Mr. Right. I did. But that was before I slept with my third first date, and definitely before I waited for a week by the phone for a call that never came. Do you know what waiting for the phone to ring will do to a person? It'll make them want to murder someone—that's what. For me, that person was him. It doesn't help matters any that there are a million and one ways to contact a person these days, and he utilized none. For fuck's sake, all it takes is a swipe of a finger. But then, that's what got him into this mess. He sideswiped the wrong girl.

It's too bad really because I sort of liked him. I honestly thought we had potential—but then I thought that about you too. Alas, it appears I was wrong, and well, you should know I've never been much good at that.

THEY SAY HISTORY REPEATS ITSELF, AND THIS IS WHY I THINK it's important to know the history of things. I've been over and over it in my mind—where I've gone wrong with these men—and I swear you have to be different. But then, I wonder if I am building you up in my mind—maybe I'm wrong about you. Maybe you will have to die too—although you seem like the kind of person who understands history.

My first date is a shy, wounded man who shows me his scars, both literally and figuratively, and if this isn't enough, he spends our date talking about his ex incessantly. But it gets worse. I kid you not—he pulls up his shirt right there in that cafe and shows me the scars from his abdominoplasty. It is strange—to say the least. But people never cease to surprise me, and isn't it a good thing to know you can still be surprised?

I guess you could say I'm coming to the realization that it's all about silver linings—this new life—this new me. Also, I'm no stranger to plastic surgery. But I never did it for love, not really. I did it because I had to be someone else.

I want to know what he knows of love, this guy, and so I go home with him, the urge to kill bubbling within me like the expensive champagne he ordered. This urge, it spills over, it threatens to pour out of me, and it almost does. But then after drinking the last of his champagne, after listening to his steady stream of bellyaching, I see it, the silver lining.

I realize "cry baby" and I do have at least one thing in common. We both know what it's like to want to be something different. Something other than what we are. This is how I know I can't kill him—even though I want to—if for nothing else to soothe my urge, but mostly, for wasting an hour and a half of my life with his whining. Then something weird happens—something weirder than him raising his shirt and showing me his surgery scars in the middle of a restaurant. I feel something I haven't felt before. And no matter how hard I try, I can't picture it in my head. I can't see myself killing him. I can't imagine how I might do it—and usually, I can see it. Maybe it's the champagne, maybe it's this new life, but suddenly, here I am like a man trying in vain to get it up. All I see are his scars, the pain he endured. I consider the price he paid, and I don't just mean the 20K he spent (yes, he *was* annoying enough to throw out the number) and I just can't picture taking all that away. He needs to own it, to own his pain, and I think he is.

This must be why I can't bring myself to use the roofies or why I can't pull my knife, even though it's there taunting me. Instead, all I can think about is how, from here on out, he'll always be the guy so afraid of his scars that he has to show them off on the first date. As though he is so unworthy of love, he might as well get it out of the way. He tells me it was all worth it, both the money and the pain, in order to be a better version of himself, and there is something about the way he lays it all out there—like a confession on Sunday—that tells me he isn't the one. Not one worth killing and not one worth a second date. So I give him a pardon. He deserves it because, this guy, he understands transformation. He understands what it takes. And maybe, I'm realizing, I do too.

DATE NUMBER TWO IS SHORT AND MEEK AND NOT AT ALL WHAT I was expecting. Not at all like the guy he portrayed in the photo. He's portly, a good decade older than his profile picture let on, and a recent divorcee who makes it clear by the time our coffees arrive that he wants someone to grow old with. He reeks of romance and good intentions—although he hardly makes eye contact and speaks only of his dog. He is weird and far too easy—not at all my type, and maybe I am very bad at picking dates.

I realize this, and I call it early. I come home and think of you, and I bet you aren't bad at dating. I bet you're very good. In fact, you're probably out with someone right now, and you're probably not thinking of me at all. The thought of it makes me want to kill someone just for the hell of it. But I'm trying to be a good girl, and so I go to the freezer and dig into a pint of Ben and Jerry's instead.

DATE NUMBER THREE—NOW—*HE* IS THE KIND WORTH KILLING. This one makes no qualms about the fact that he was only looking for a good time. He confirms the suspicion that I am indeed bad at love. Also, I mess up, and I sleep with him. I mistakenly think sex will soothe the urge to kill—but in this case, it only makes it worse.

The sex is good, he had a great ass, and even though afterward, I lie there thinking of you, I figure with an ass like that he can certainly serve as a temporary distraction. I figure he could be my 'in the meantime.'

Until he doesn't call. Until he uses me and turns me out like I'm nothing more than a two dollar whore.

Until it's time to do something about it, and I have to admit, the plotting—the imagining—it helps.

I'VE BEEN RUNNING FOR SO LONG NOW, I'M NOT SURE I KNOW how to stop. The world isn't safe for a girl like me. That's what my father always said, and it's the irony of this I consider as I simultaneously listen to the footsteps behind me as they hit the pavement, and I do my best to study the rhythm of them as one by one they match mine. Judging the weight by the thud with which they hit the ground, I know without a doubt they belong to a man.

Why this man is following me, I'm not quite sure. I think of you for a moment, and I wonder if it could be, but then why would you find me here, and why like this? In any case, why doesn't exactly matter at 2:38 in the morning when you're in a dark, dank, empty—aside from the two of you—alley. In this case, *why* becomes irrelevant, because whatever the reason, you know it certainly can't be anything good.

This is nice, I think, as I tighten my grip around the base of the knife. I steady my breath, and as I run the coolness of the blade across my fingertip, I audibly exhale. On my next inhale, I mentally prepare myself for what comes next, and then I slow my pace and wait.

I listen as he slows too and switches up his pace. But with each step forward, I sense him there, lurking in the shadows not far behind, just as I was trying to do, and the thought of him watching excites me.

I can feel he's holding back while I'm ready to get on with it, and so I stop abruptly and turn—only there's no one there. At least, not that I can see.

But he's there. I can feel him.

For a second, I'm angry, and I imagine taking my blade and shoving it into his hesitant little neck, twisting slightly on the way in. Because whoever he is—he's rudely interrupting my plans, and he's being sloppy about it to boot. He shouldn't be here. He shouldn't be following me—I'm not here to kill *him*—this blade has someone else's name written on it—someone who had already spun himself too far into my web to break loose now. And, in roughly seven minutes and eighteen seconds, that someone is due to come walking down this alley as he does every Thursday in the early hours of the morning. And damn it if this asshole and his ill intent aren't throwing a wrench in everything and forcing my hand in a way I never wanted it to go.

Taking a step backward, I search the corners where the light from the streetlamp almost touches. Still, I see nothing. But he's there. I know it.

Carefully, I begin to turn. I figure if he won't come to me, then I'll go to him, and this is when I feel him closing in. I firmly adjust the base of the knife in my palm, strengthening my grip, and suddenly, his hands are on me. With one hand clasped against my mouth, the other around my neck, he's dragging me backward.

This isn't how this was supposed to go, I think, and I buck against him using my bodyweight before attempting to ram my foot into his shin. Only, he's quick, and he dodges it, and I'm not making any headway at getting free. Instinctively, I bring my knife around my body where I plan to plunge it into the arm that's draped around my neck. But then he releases my mouth and deftly takes the knife from my hand as something inaudible escapes my lips. Not quite a scream, not quite a growl, and I can't lose this fight—I won't. We are dancing, and he is leading, and I don't like to be led, and this is how I know it's time for a change of tune.

I decide then I'll let him think he's getting his way. It'll be his penance as I make him beg for his life while killing him slowly. The thought of redemption is thrilling, so I smile and go limp, and in turn, he proceeds as I had expected when he spins me around and pins me backward against the wall. The cool brick feels nice against my skin. I feel everything, and it warms me from the inside out—from the moonless sky to the absence of breath in the air, I feel it all. I feel the radio silence of this night all the way to my bones. The darkness is chilling, and I feel that too, but I'm not fighting him. Instead, I work within his swift movements, attempting to get a look at his face, but he's wearing a mask and doesn't stay still long enough for me to make anything out. So I'll just have to focus his attention.

"Whatever you want, take it," I say to him, and I know he has to die.

He hesitates then as though he's unsure of what should happen next, and in his misstep, I bring my knee up hard into his groin. He takes it surprisingly well, not completely doubling over as they usually do. How unexpected, I think, and this is when I'm interrupted by laughter. Thankfully, not his. I turn my head in the direction of the sound, and if I squint hard enough, I'm certain I can faintly make out the outline of a group of people heading our way.

"Damn it," I spit and he is on me again. Pinned against the weight of his body, I realize I'm useless until he decides to make another move. Only he doesn't. Instead, ever so gently

—gently enough that it makes it awkward, he takes a strand of my hair between his fingers and threads it through, letting it fall back to my shoulder, watching all the while as it does. Then he leans in close, close enough I can't see his eyes, even though I try. I'm just about to make my move—but we are having a moment—when he takes my ponytail and grips it hard, twisting it around his fist. In the light that filters through the shadow, I can see he's shaking his head.

"Not tonight," he croons, and his voice is low and rough. Sexy.

My eyes burn from trying so hard to focus, and my throat is closed and too dry to speak—when he releases me, and backs away gradually. I'm not ready to give up. I want a fight, I'm prepared for a fight, but instead, he's telling me to go—or else he'll kill me. He opens his jacket, and he brandishes a handgun, and there's a small part of me that believes him, so I turn and run. Not because I'm afraid—but because running is what I know and because I've come too far to stop now.

After I've rounded the nearest corner, I double over, and after a futile attempt to catch my breath, I turn back and see my attacker is conversing with the men. They're closer now than before, and although I can't hear what is being said, I *can* make out that my target is among the mix.

Waiting for their little powwow to end, I hang around for a second, although I might've waited forever, and before I know it, the men continue on in my direction. I want to follow the plan, I want to ask for directions, and then pull a stab and run, but instead, I watch as 'Mr. Not Tonight' slips back into the shadows, and I do the same, knowing he's watching, knowing it's too risky, and hating that he's right—that I won't get my kill tonight.

As I retreat toward the confines of my car, I watch my back, feeling hopeful for more, and as the warm air brushes against the cool sweaty skin I want to crawl out of, I'm annoyed that it's come to this. The night air shouldn't feel this temperate because this night is ruined forever. There's no hope, no getting it back, no making it right, and now that I've given in, even the weather seems to be taunting me, teaching me a lesson on perfection, showing me all the ways I'm lacking. I watch as late-night partygoers disperse into the darkness. They're happier than they have the right to be, and I'm irritated by their indifference. Life isn't fair, and it isn't just because I've come up empty-handed. More so because I'm afraid it will be a long time before I'll understand why the stranger in the dark did what he did—and what it was he meant by his words.

But I need to.

I have to.

The good news is—it isn't over.

I know because he could've killed me if he'd wanted to.

And here I am. Still alive.

Dying to tell you.

CHAPTER SEVEN

JUDE

I arrive twenty minutes early for our date. It's important to get a feel for a place. This is just one reason among many I'm a believer in being early. For one, it's a strategic move. It puts the person you're meeting at a disadvantage from the get go. It may be subconscious on their part—but they're late, even when they're not—and just like that, already you're ahead.

Always stay two steps ahead. Rudy taught me that. Speaking of staying two steps ahead, you should really give this some thought, and then guys like me wouldn't have to save your ass in dark alleys. Jesus, Kate. You're impulsive, and impulsiveness will either get you caught or dead. I don't know if our first date is the place to let you in on this, but I know one thing—neither can happen before I've seen you naked.

I've spent the last five minutes in the parking lot mulling this over while watching the patrons entering and exiting, and not one of them, I imagine, would look as good as you without clothes on. I look for you, but knowing you, you're the type to show up late, and fashionably so, if I believed in such a thing. I don't. Late is just another word for rude.

With fifteen minutes to spare and no sign of you or anyone even remotely interesting, I give up and enter the restaurant. I contemplate waiting outside, but it's early June, and Texas is making it unbearable, and I don't want to stink when you show up. Inside, the hostess offers a menu while I wait and I decline. I don't tell her I've already studied it, and I know exactly what I plan to order because not everything needs to be said. Instead, I wait, and I watch.

I've prepared well so I'm expecting nothing but good things. At lunchtime, I called our dinner reservation in and requested a private table—it's our anniversary, or so I told the hostess who took my call. She seemed excited for us, as though this isn't a conversation she has umpteen times a day, and it's nice to know others love their work too.

I bet you love your work, and I plan to find out if I'm right. Like you, this place is darker than I thought. There's a man playing the piano somewhere as though his life depends on it and I should have come for lunch. I should have gotten a feel for the place, a sentiment that only multiplies when another hostess arrives on the scene, presumably the one who enjoys her job and informs me that you're already waiting. You're seated at the bar, she says. *Of course, you are.*

As she leads me in your direction, I spot you instantly. There's a glass of water in front of you, which you clearly haven't touched, and for some reason, this makes me smile. I size you up in your dark skinny jeans and slinky top—you look amazing, and I like that you've dressed up for me. The look you're going for is sexy but aloof. I can tell by the way your chestnut hair hangs low against the back of the barstool. I can tell by the way your eyes linger when ever so slightly you turn in my direction, and you throw your head back in full on laughter. I can tell by the way you look away first, as though there's a joke I'm not quite in on yet.

It doesn't take long to see the joke happens to be courtesy of the businessman seated to your right, and I will smash his face in if he ever makes you laugh like that again. It seems silly given that we hardly know each other, but from this moment on, I want that job, and I won't let anyone stand in my way of getting it.

The hostess stops a few feet shy of you and motions in my direction. "Ryan?" you say, and your laugh fades, your smile goes with it, and you look confused.

"That's me," I answer. I smile at you genuinely as I extend my hand. I settle matters when I briefly turn my gaze to the guy seated to your right, and I raise my eyebrows, but I do not smile. See, she's with me, the look says, and you don't seem to notice. I feel you studying my face, and it doesn't go unnoticed that you don't take my hand. But I like that you don't immediately trust. It pleases me that you aren't one of those girls.

But then you lean in for a hug, and it catches me off guard, the way your body presses against mine. You whisper, "Thank God," and your mouth is so close to my ear, and there's no going back from here. "I'm Kate," you tell me, introducing yourself, but I know this, I've learned a thing or two. In my mind, we've already met, even if not officially, and your poker face could use some improvement. My breath catches in my throat when your lips brush against my skin, and it sends chills down my spine. The hostess makes a noise from the back of her throat, something between a cough and a word, and it's clear we're wasting her time, and now I wish she loved her job more. Clearly, she doesn't know a good greeting when she sees one, and so I swallow hard and then pull away slowly. I let you slip by first so I can check out your ass in those jeans. You seem happy to oblige when I usher you in the direction of the hostess. Your ass looks great, by the way, and my hand feels that way as it just barely grazes the small of your back, leading you where I want you to go.

The hostess pulls out your chair, a small shot at redemption in my book, and I wait for you to take your seat because I want you to know I am a gentleman. But also because I want more time to check you out.

It's loud in here, and I wish it were just you and I. We don't need an audience, Kate. That's not our style. The place is crowded, I tell you—especially for a weeknight—and you agree, and already, I can tell we're two of a kind.

You don't like trivial conversation, either. I can tell by the look on your face. You make me nervous, and nothing ever does, and so I make small talk to ease us into the rest of our lives. The truth is, I haven't a clue whether this place is really busy or whether this is normal. I don't say this, but unless I'm tailing a subject, I rarely go out on weeknights—or any other night, for that matter. But I won't tell you this because sometimes the truth is worth keeping to yourself.

A waiter, presumably ours, places two glasses of water on the table, and you look at me. Your eyes, they tell a story, and it's one I want to know. You order a glass of white while I stick to water, and then there's silence, which you try to fill, and this is how I know you like me too.

"I've been here once," you say, and you smile as you say it, but just barely. It doesn't touch those eyes of yours. "A long time ago."

I nod, and suddenly, you seem far off, and it's too early to ask about the past, so I just stare at the menu. This is the first time it hurts to look at you. It won't be the last.

"You don't drink?" you ask and your voice, it's like the rest of you, it demands my attention. You want it solely on you, and this is good.

"No," I tell you, meeting your gaze.

You purse your lips although your expression gives little away. You're harder to read than I thought. I can't tell if my answer was the one you were looking for, but you are a mystery I look forward to figuring out.

"My mother was an alcoholic," I tell you. The words slip out too easily, burning as they pass over my tongue. I shouldn't have said this, and immediately, I wish words were something you could pull back in.

"My father is too," you tell me, and something changes in your eyes. "Or, well, I guess I should say, my father *was* an alcoholic."

"Are you saying you have a drinking problem?" I ask. I give being a smartass a shot because you used the word too, lumping yourself into a category in which you don't belong, and I pay attention to words. They're important. I want you to know this, but it isn't why I act like a dick. It's because I'd do just about anything to get us off on another foot. Parents are never the best place to start with a date. Only now, I hate myself, and why did I just say this because you don't get my lame attempt at humor, and I can't help but be disappointed when you don't laugh, and I think you have lost interest. Until you surprise me by raising your glass. "Not yet," you say.

"Well, then you have something to aspire to," I say, and you smile then, and I love that you're a smartass too.

"Cheers," you say as you clink your glass to mine. You offer a wry smile and still, I detect a hint of disappointment.

"I'm sorry," I tell you. "It's just that I don't do this often..."

"Converse?" you ask, and you take another sip of your wine. You're testing me to see if I can hang, and I assure you I can. I can tell by the way you peer over that glass at me with those fuck me eyes that we're heading into the danger zone. You know it, and I know it, and you are good at flirting.

I smile. "Date," I tell you, and I will show you where my experience lies. I can promise you—it is not in a restaurant making small talk.

"Wait," you whisper, looking around. When you turn your attention back to me, where it belongs, you lower your voice, "So this is a date?" You don't wait for the next non-brilliant smartass thing I have to say. You raise your brow, and you jut your bottom lip out ever so slightly until I'm consumed with the need to take it between my teeth. I promise you something else, although not out loud—when we get out of here, I intend to do just that.

For now, I simply shrug. But I think you know what I'm thinking. I think you're thinking it too because you grin. I watch as it slips away just as quickly as it appeared.

You take a deep breath and let it out. "Because you could've fooled me," you say, and you then smile, wryly. "Here I thought I was here for an interrogation."

And then, suddenly, I'm grinning too. Because I like you. Because you're good. But, also, because you don't even know the half of it.

AFTER DINNER, I TAKE YOU BACK TO MY PLACE. WE LEAVE your car at the restaurant, and you really should know better than to get in the car with men you hardly know.

Apparently, you don't—but then you can't know how easy you are making my job. I could so easily drive you to the police station right now and turn you in. It would be so simple to collect my money without passing go.

But Kate, the problem is, I want to pass go. I want you in my bed—or wherever—I want to know if you feel what I'm feeling, and then we'll pass go. I want to fuck you just to say I've done it—I want to do it because I can. Maybe this makes me an asshole, but I've never pretended to be anything else.

"I've never done this before," you say reading my mind. You're surveying my kitchen, sizing me up, and you're a bad little liar, you are.

"Me either," I tell you, and I am not lying because I'm referring to fucking someone I've been hired to turn over to the cops. This lie comes easy because most criminals are men and the ones who aren't, never looked like you. But then you're referring to one-night stands, not fucking criminals, and I'd be willing to bet you're more experienced than you're letting on where that's concerned.

I find this thought disturbing, and I shake my head as though it will rattle loose and get lost, and you notice and cock your head. I don't like to think about the things you've done before because, quite frankly, it's a buzz kill. Your eyes meet mine, and I swear your tits perk up when you smile, and I can forgive your mistakes, for now. Because when you know what you want, you know what you want, and this makes it pretty simple. And I'm not one to turn down that which is easy.

You saunter over to me as though you're telepathic, and you make your move. You don't wait for me to offer you a drink—which is good because I don't have anything but water. You're impatient, and I like this about you. You slip your hand underneath my shirt, and you run your finger along my skin, killing me slowly, just a little more as you make your way up my chest. When I can't take it anymore, I pull you in closer. You purr like a kitten, and you don't stop when I cover your mouth with mine. In an instant, you make me impatient too, and my hands are everywhere, and you are a needy little thing. Your body begs for more—it's your tell, it gives you away.

But then you pull away and what the hell?

"Don't you think we should talk a bit first?" you stammer, but your eyes are hungry—they don't lie. You're filled with need, and I am good at reading people, Kate. You don't want to talk. You want me to pin you against the wall and peel you out of those jeans. You want to see my head buried between your thighs. You want to watch as I thrust into you.

"Who needs words?" I ask, moving in to do just that.

You put your palm up, pressing it to my chest and you stop me. You push back hard, and maybe you want it rough, but it's too early in the game for that.

"I think we should talk about the future," you say, but I can tell you are toying with me. Your eyes linger, and we both know talking isn't what you came here for. Your face is flush, and your lips are wet, and you're full of shit, and this turns me on more than you could ever know.

"Well," I start, more determined than ever, and I'll talk the whole way through if you want. But I don't take you for one of those girls although I'm willing to call your bluff. "First, I'm going to peel those jeans off and then I'm going to—"

"Right," you say interrupting me, and I was trying to tell you your future. But I was right. You aren't a talker, and maybe you don't like foreplay—and why are we still talking? "But what happens after?" you want to know. You're biting your lip, and your eyes cut holes in me. You are a bad girl, and I will make you pay.

"That depends on how good the sex is," I say, and I am honest, and maybe honesty is your brand of foreplay because suddenly, your hand is pressed against my mouth. You want me to just get on with it, I can tell by the way your eyes bore into mine. Next thing I know, you are pulling off my shirt, and I am tugging at your jeans, and then I am inside of you. But you're inside of me too, even though I have you pinned against the counter. You are everywhere, and I never knew a person could taste so good. You bite my lip, and the harder I thrust, the harder you bite. I taste blood, and you beg for more, but how much is too much? I don't know yet, but I'm willing to learn.

I give you what you want, and I hope it's enough because I give you everything I have until we're both lying on my kitchen floor, sweaty and spent. I've never liked this kitchen more.

Later, in the haze of what we've done, I bring up the future just like you wanted when I tell you it was the best sex of my life. I'm not lying, and you say you know, and then we do it again, just to make sure. Unsurprisingly, the second time is even better, and this is so good... until I remember, it's bad.

"It's a short fall to the bottom," you say, and how is it you always know what I'm thinking?

"I know," I tell you as I cup your breast. I don't tell you that I was happy to learn they weren't fake, that I thanked a god I don't believe in, and still, I can't help but wonder how much of this, how much of you, is real.

"This could get addictive," you add. Your head is in my lap, your breath labored, and I wonder if you'll go or if you'll stay.

"It could," I agree, and I know because there's no going back from here. There's no way of not knowing what it feels like to be inside you. I've taken that first hit, and then a second, and now it seems my fate is sealed. I am a junkie, no better and no worse than any other kind, and we have a problem. The only upside is I never knew a problem could feel this good.

CHAPTER EIGHT

KATE

It was you in that alley. I know it immediately. Ok, well, maybe not *immediately,* but it is clear the moment I place my hands on your chest in your kitchen. I know by the way you feel, and I know by the way you smell. I don't tell you I know because this is not a time for talking.

I have to have you, not just tonight, but indefinitely. Or at the very least, for this lifetime—this much I also know. You found me, as I knew you would, and when I least expected it, you showed up and called yourself my date. This in and of itself would have been enough. But then you invite me into your home, your bed, your heart, in a way that leaves little doubt that I will be inexplicably changed for having known you.

After we've made love for the third time, we lie together in your bed, too blissful and too tired for sleep. I want to know you, inside and out. I ask if you've ever been in love, and you laugh and tell me yes. Right now, you say, in this very moment, and I smile, even though we both know it's too soon for bold declarations. I like your sense of humor. I find the way you bullshit endearing. It's like a second language we speak that only the other understands. It's a rare quality to know this foreign language we speak otherwise known as the art of bullshitting. Most people never pick it up.

I dig and prod a little, and you tell me about your first love, Amy, and there's nothing like the first, this I know for sure. You tell me how you met her in Sri Lanka, and I tell you I've never been. It's a beautiful country, you say, and I feel silly for being the odd one out. Maybe we should go. I interrupt you and tell you this, and you smile sardonically. But I can tell you don't think I'm crazy, and it is nice that you simply continue on with your story.

You were sixteen, she was nineteen. She was a Londoner, taking a gap year. You were there with your dad for work. Her name was Amy, and she was blonde and beautiful—worldly and, unlike you, not the least bit shy. You talked about books and far away galaxies and friends back home, everything and nothing important—existential conversation —the kind best had with strangers.

Later, under the stars, she would kiss you before slipping her hand beneath your shorts and then you wouldn't be strangers anymore. You still remember the look in her eye when you told her you'd never. It's better that way, she told you, and then she taught you what it means to please a woman. For six days, she was your teacher, and in the end, you say, forever your lesson. I want to hate her, and I do, but I will admit, she taught you well.

You wrote letters to each other for three years. She told you of her travels, and then her studies abroad. You told her of life in Texas. You made things up because you couldn't stand to tell her the truth. It was one of the most creative periods in your life, you admit. You fell in love with an almost stranger and her words. You invented yourself for her, because of her, and you believed in the person she made you become. That is, until one day without warning, the letters stopped. Your eyes turn sad when you tell me how you went over and over the last letter she wrote, over the last letter you sent, trying to find something—a sign—anything to explain why she vanished from your life. But there was nothing you could pinpoint, and for this, I hate her more. Everyone needs closure, and you may have missed the point, but I surely didn't. She knew exactly what she was doing by leaving you hanging. She was giving herself a way back in.

You can't see this, though, not yet. You'll never know what happened, you tell me, if Amy got sick and died, or if it was a car accident or whether she simply met someone else and changed her mind. The last of your correspondence said she was settling back near the place you met, and you agreed to visit, but then the letters stopped. It hurt like hell at the time, the wondering nearly drove you insane you admit, but now that you're older and wiser, you find the whole thing really quite beautiful. She changed her mind about you, in any case, and what more was there to say? A lot, I almost tell you. But I don't.

I tell you we should find her, and if she isn't dead, we should make it happen. For being cold-hearted, for breaking your heart the way she did. You laugh because you think I'm making a joke, and I smile because I'm not. What an adventure, don't you think, tracking down one's first love and making them pay? You say yes, and I can't tell if you're serious. But then you tell me you like adventure, and I believe you.

YOU TOLD ME BY CANDLELIGHT LAST NIGHT THAT YOUR REAL name is not Ryan as it said on the dating site, as you said at dinner. It's Jude. I wasn't surprised. We all become someone different online. As you ran the tips of your fingers across my cheek, you promised you were sorry for lying, and then you showed me when you touched my scars with your lips. You asked for the truth about them, but I didn't give it to you. You don't get to be the only one who lies. Which is why I haven't told you exactly who or what I am. It isn't time for whole truths about anything.

Speaking of names, it took a lot to pry Amy's last name from your lips, and you see... you do still keep her close to your heart. You're protecting her. This is how I know. It's dangerous, Jude. *She* is dangerous, and you need closure, you really do. It's too much to go around carrying the weight of her, believe me, I know. Morris was the answer you gave when you finally relented. But you lied. Your jaw did this twitchy thing, and that's how I knew. We all have our tells, and apparently, that's yours.

"No doubt, she's married now," you add, to cover your tracks, to conceal your lies, and you are still in denial, still protecting her, and it's okay because, luckily, I know how to hunt people.

I withdrew in your lies, and you sensed me pull away.

I started slowly at first, retreating into myself and then I left and didn't speak to you for four days. You let me have my space, at first. I'll give you that. But the thing you need to know about women is that it isn't space we want, not really. We want a fight. We want a man willing to burn for us— someone willing to put it all on the line. We want to go to war.

I know you have it in you, I do. This is why I don't return your calls. This is why I play hard to get when the truth is I miss you. I miss the way your arms feel around me, the way your eyes bore holes into my soul—all the ways you seem to know me even though you don't. So on the fourth day, when you show up at my door, this is why I practically leap into your arms. You aren't confused like most men would be. Not you. You come bearing gifts that aren't flowers. You come bearing breakfast and plane tickets, and you are a warrior, Jude, you are. When I kiss you, to show you you're forgiven, you taste like bacon and syrup. You taste like my future.

TWO DAYS LATER WE'RE ON A PLANE BOUND FOR SRI LANKA. You sleep while I stare out the window, into the clouds, and I wonder how I'll do it. I hope Amy isn't alive, so I don't have to kill this first love of yours. But the sad truth is you can't fall in love with a person if you're still pining after another.

We need a clean start, and also, there's the simple fact she broke your heart. People need to learn they can't go around ruining people's lives, soiling their hearts for others, cheapening what it means to love. People like Amy need to know they can't get away with it. There has to be justice for taking something as pure as love from a person and causing so much pain in return. I saw the look in your eye when you told me about her. I know you loved this Amy and, worse yet, I know you still do. How could you not? You need closure, and I couldn't do anything about the look of sadness in your eye, but I can do something about this.

Maybe we do need a little adventure, you said. It would be nice to see a contact you have there, you admitted. But when I ask if it's one of your banking contacts, you're all out of lies, and so you lead with the truth. You tell me that you aren't really a banker—that you're a hit man, and I laugh at first, but then I believe you, because, of course, you are. Turns out, you're more than I thought. You kill people for money, and I do too. I don't tell you this, right then, even though I want to. Instead, I kiss you and slowly let the moment pass.

But soon. Soon, we'll get everything out in the open, and

there will be nothing standing between us—no more secrets, and most importantly, no more Amy.

WE HIT TURBULENCE, IN MORE WAYS THAN ONE, AND YOU ARE awake. Also, we have assholes seated across from us who are at it again, and I am determined to fix this. This trip, it is the start of something, the beginning of us, and I will not let it be ruined by incessant, whiny people who refuse to shut up. This woman. She prays and she prays, and I swear I've never seen anything quite like it. She's got stamina, I'll give her that. Not even when I clearly offered my best stink eye did she cease with the praying. It's loud too, as though she wants an audience, as though the more people hear, the greater the odds her God is listening. I think we're going on three hundred Hail Marys by this point, and we still have a ways to go. Obviously, she finds prayer comforting. I find it disturbing, and yet when I complain to the flight attendant, she looks at me as though I'm the weird one. It's nonstop. She prays, her husband shushes her, they argue, and then she goes back to praying. It's never-ending, their bickering, and I tell you that is not love, and I hope you don't get the wrong idea about marriage. Love would be putting the lady out of her misery in order to save the rest of us. That's *real* sacrifice. You laugh when I say this, and I'm not sure why. Nothing is funny.

These people are insufferable. They're bored with life, and we will never be them. I know their type—I've seen this all before. When you reside in resort towns, you see a lot. Vacation tends to bring out the best and the worst in people. Also, you can't really know a person until you've traveled with them. But I know this kind well, and unfortunately, by mere chance, we're traveling with them, and we're trapped in this metal container with only one way out, which, at the moment, just so happens to be sudden death.

Nonetheless, the alternative is WASPs who incessantly blame one another for all the shortcomings of their bloated, middle-aged lives. I'm not sure it gets much worse for them than being trapped in a metal vessel together, for hours on end, one which will inevitably hurl them back toward a home they can't stand. This is why they have nothing better to do than bicker until one of them cries uncle and agrees that the other is right—until they profess everything is their fault. Not that it even matters. They're one and the same— hell, these people even look alike. But given her pleas to God, if I were the betting kind, I'd place my money on the husband calling it in first. Still, I don't see him leaving alto- gether. He's invested too much in this shitty dynamic. He secretly gets off on it, I can tell.

Not that I'm an expert on relationships or anything. Aside from once, a long time ago, I've never been one-half of a pair, and you should know, it was nothing like this. Given this fact, I have no idea how long this can go on, the prayer, the meaningless back and forth exchange between the two of them, but I swear to you if it doesn't stop soon—someone may die.

Just when I begin to think it's going to happen sooner rather than later, the flight attendant brings us drinks even though we haven't asked. Maybe she gets it after all. When you get up to use the lavatory, I offer mine to the prayer lady, but not before slipping a little something magical into it.

I silently pray it helps her mouth issue quickly, but she thumbs her nose at my offering, and I should've known not to waste my best stuff on her. I should have read her better— she prays—*not drinks,* and this is a disaster. Her other half, however, surprises me when he leans over and takes the cocktail from my hand. He offers thanks, and he is the smart one.

I almost tell the man I should be drinking it but that I'm with you, and I don't want to miss a thing, so I'm taking one for the team. But we aren't a team, he and I. In fact, at this moment, I hate his very existence. I hate that he'll probably drink my drink, and he'll know peace while the rest of us will go on suffering.

You give me the once over when you return to your seat, and I swear it's like you know what I've done.

"You and I will never be like them," you say, and you reach for my hand. You're a mind reader, and it doesn't get any better than this.

"I know," I tell you, intertwining my hand in yours.

"Breathe," you whisper, and I exhale.

You squeeze my hand, and I squeeze back. We don't talk. You and I, we understand the value of silence. It's golden.

Eventually, you hand me your drink, and you know me well.

You speak my language. Even without words.

CHAPTER NINE

JUDE

You seduce me in your sleep. It's interesting, this turn of events, being here, with you, on a plane bound for a place I made up. Sri Lanka is real, obviously, but that's not the point. Amy is real, too. But I did not meet her there, and as far as I know, she's never been. It's ok, though. This is what makes it so fascinating. The fact you suggested this trip because you're convinced we need to find the girl who broke my heart, well, this is how I know you're for real, and I almost want to wake you to tell you this.

I want to tell you all the things I don't tell anyone, but instead, I let you dream.

I watch your chest rise and fall as I silently count your breaths. I want to know all of you, and you look beautiful passed out beside me. You're in a deep sleep, and you don't mind me watching, thanks to the liquor and the sleeping pills. Your eyelids flutter, you're dreaming, and I hope it's about me. You think the flight attendant was being nice, and that's cute because it's important you believe in the good in this world. But there's a facade you miss, smoke and mirrors, and you will learn. Or maybe you won't, and this thought is kind of nice too. I bought those drinks, and I slipped something extra in to save you from the dreadful people across the aisle. We are so lucky to have found each other, Kate. We're two of a kind. I know you drugged that man, same as I drugged you, and this is how I know I'll never be able to complete this job. This is how I know I'll never be able to turn you in.

We land and it's tough to wake you, but I manage, and you are groggy, and you're pissed, and I think it's because you know. Or maybe you're always like this when you wake, but it's too soon to know. We have a problem, though, and it's a big one. The guy across the aisle, he's proving tougher to wake than you. In fact, he doesn't wake at all, and now we have ourselves a dead man.

The good news is, it's equally our fault this guy is dead. You know it by the way you feel. You sense you've been drugged, and I know it because I saw you slip that powder into his drink, all the while I knew I'd first added my own.

You seem irritated with me, but maybe it's just the drugs. The best part is we have time to find out. You won't call me out on it, not now, not yet. Later on—down the road, I'm certain, you won't hesitate—but here and now, in the newness of this relationship, you aren't completely sure that you've been deceived, and so you let it slide. This is why beginnings are nice, Kate. Because in the beginning, people appreciate what is. For now, you appreciate a good nap, and you don't question the specifics. I don't know if it's possible to keep things this way, but I believe we can. I believe in us.

When we finally deplane, I buy you water, and you watch me open it, and it's funny. It seems like you don't quite trust me. It doesn't matter, though. I shrug it off because all things can be taught, and by the time we arrive at our hotel, you're over it. You're resilient that way, Kate.

After we get checked in and settled in our room, I head straight for the shower. I don't ask you to join me. I know better. I've done this a time or two, and so I wait and let you come to me. I don't want to rush this. I want you to open up for me. I want to watch you bloom, I want you to trust me, and I'm certain you will. And then, just like that, you do. Space is good for women, I find. It makes them grateful. You seem to agree without saying as much. When you finally come to me, I press you against the shower wall, against the glass, and give you what you need to forgive me. We let our bodies do the talking and love is the language we speak.

Later, you lie across the bed, and you watch me dress. I'm jet-lagged, but you aren't. You're playful. You've been on your phone looking for Amy. I ask what you're reading, and you tell me so matter of factly, as though your mission for revenge is the sole reason we've come.

"I don't care about Amy...I'm not here with her," I tell you and my voice has an edge. I wonder how well you want to get to know that edge, if you plan to slip over but you don't. We both realize my words come out more harshly than I meant them to. I can tell by the way you look up and meet my eye.

You stare for a while. I ignore you as I unpack. You're being needy, the way most women are after sex, and I will not feed your addiction by giving you my attention. Instead, I put things away. You pout. You want to talk about my ex. I want you to let it go, and I wonder how long these power struggles can go on.

"You're very organized," you offer up eventually, and then you roll over onto your back and let out a long sigh. I watch as you stretch out, twist over onto one side and then the other, and I swear you're testing me. You're greedy, and I look away. When I look up again, I can't help it, you've slipped out of your robe, and you lie there naked. You know how to get what you want, you do. You have my attention, and I am captivated. I want to photograph you in this light, and I wonder if it's too soon to ask. I could keep you here forever like this, my little pet. You watch me hang the last of my shirts, and you stretch out again, settle in. "Tell me, Jude —" you say, "where do you think all this is going?"

"What do you mean?" I ask even though I know exactly what you mean. You want a crystal ball. You want to know the future. But I'm not a fortune teller. Not yet.

"I mean…what do you want out of life…" you ask, and you sigh again. "You know—where do you see yourself in five years—that sorta thing…"

I raise my brow. You're going to play that angle, huh? "So —let's be clear here," I tell you only halfway serious. "What you're really asking is whether or not I see a future with you in it."

You bite your lip, you seem embarrassed for having asked, and that was exactly the point. You should be embarrassed. You don't even know me. Right now, I don't even know myself. I know because I go to you, and I run the backside of my hand across your belly. Your skin flushes and maybe I've been too hard on you. I hover over you, and you relax into the bed, into my touch, and it suits you having my full attention. You're comfortable in my hands—you like knowing I'm in control.

"No, actually," you whisper, now that you have me where you want me. "I was just curious whether or not we want the same things…"

I stroke your breast and I know what I want. "What is it you want?" I ask, taking your left nipple between my forefinger and thumb. I pinch hard. Obviously not hard enough, because you only grin.

"This," you purr. "And more."

My eyes are on yours. You are bad for me and so good too. I squeeze your other nipple "How much more?"

"I want it all..." you say, and you exhale. You look away, and you're far off, you're there, wherever there is. "Babies... a house in a neighborhood... dinner with friends on Friday nights and... maybe even a dog."

I swallow and then raise my brow. "Then you should have that."

You smile, and you curve your body toward me, and it's as though you're a magnet pulling me in. "I'm working on it," you tell me and you are.

"Hmm," I murmur stroking your inner thighs. You almost whimper, and you will before I'm done. You slither like a snake under my touch. I offer the best I've got, and I think, for you, I always will. "What do you say we work together?"

You grin, and you make your move. I watch as you pull back the sheets. You pat the spot next to you—you reel me in. "Sounds like a plan," you say, as I slip between the sheets and into the future.

~

"GET DRESSED," I URGE YOU, SHAKING YOU AWAKE. WE'VE overslept, and this is bad. "We have to go," I tell you, pulling on my clothes. "Bob despises all forms of tardiness."

"Who's Bob," you ask when you finally climb out of bed. You're slow in the mornings. I know this now.

"Bob is my contact here," I inform you. You offer me a blank stare, and I realize getting out of here is going to require more handholding than I thought. I reach down to grab a pair of jeans from your half-open luggage, and I throw them in your direction.

"What does that even mean?" you sigh, and I swear, you are chaos. We're late, clearly, and you need to know I've never done well with disorder.

"It means we're late. And I don't like being late. It's rude," I seethe as I search for what I need.

"Late for what?" you demand, and you ask too many questions.

"For training."

"Training? What kind of training?" you ask, and you want to know everything. I want to scream at you. You make me furious, and I want to take you by the arm to dress you like a child, and I almost do. But when I come out of the bathroom, I'm pleased to see that you're sliding into your jeans and you make me curious too. You go commando, and it's exactly *that* kind of training, I want to tell you. But you are a woman, and well, you are you, and I realize this will only lead to more questions.

"The kind we're late for," I tell you instead. You can't find your other shoe. I hold the door open and wait. People pass by, they gawk; they can't help it. You're still only half-dressed, and you're trying, you are. But I can see we have a long way to go.

WE GET IN A TUK. YOU AREN'T SURE ABOUT THIS METHOD OF travel, but I can tell you're intrigued. The tuk takes us to Bob's place. Bob resides on the outskirts of town, and it's funny how nothing looks as I remember it, and yet everything feels the same. You don't ask questions. You're quieter than I've ever seen you. I study your profile. This country mesmerizes you with its beauty, and I am mesmerized by you.

I spent several summers here, I tell you, watching your face. You don't look at me, and I add that I spent them with Bob. I can't wait for you to meet him, I say, but you only stare. Nothing changes in your profile, but I can't help but notice the way your bottom lip juts out ever so slightly. You don't reply. You haven't replied to anything I've said since we left the hotel, and I want to know what you are thinking. I want to know everything about you. I want you to know most things about me.

Later, I tell you that Bob is an old Special Forces friend of my father's. I tell you Bob taught me everything I know. He taught me everything Rudy didn't. We started with martial arts before moving onto the art of breaking and entering—but mostly, Bob taught me how to snipe. He taught me to be an expert marksman. I don't tell you this. I plan to show you.

That's what we're here for today. Or at least partly. Mostly, we're here because I need Bob's opinion of you. I need it for my own peace of mind, and for sure, I'll need it for my father when he finds out you aren't just a girlfriend—but a job. I'll appease him, some by telling him that I've taken you to meet Bob. He's an expert at reading people—my father knows this as well as anyone, and he respects his opinion. But then, everyone respects Bob's opinion it seems. He was a spy in another life, among other things. Things, I should add, he never talks about.

I explain to you that he was like a second father to me, and I don't have to tell you that his opinion matters. You know, and you don't ask questions. You simply watch the blur of people as we race toward our fortuneteller.

WE HAVE LUNCH WITH BOB. YOU ASK QUESTIONS ABOUT HIS life—about why he lives here in Sri Lanka, and he is surprisingly candid with you about it all. He loves the people here—that's what he told you, and that is mostly the truth. The rest of it being that Bob is a retired hit man. There's a huge bounty on his head, making him a very wanted man, and in turn, he finds this remote island a good place to hide out. That much, he doesn't share. Even so, he's the most openly friendly, incredibly private person I've ever met. Bob is a man who has mastered the art of hiding in plain sight. Not that he's hiding here, per se. He just doesn't go looking for trouble.

After lunch, he shows you around the farm. He shares a few stories of my visits over the years, and as he does, he goes in for the kill.

"What do you know of hunting, Kate?" he asks you, opening his gun safe.

"Frankly, not much," you tell him.

He purses his lips and retrieves what he went in for. "Well, I certainly hope you're a better shot than you are a liar," he replies, and you flash a smile that slays.

Bob hands me a gun, and then he takes one for himself. Then he closes and locks the safe. You sulk, the odd woman out, and I appease you by telling you that I'll share.

Bob is punishing you for lying to him. He hates liars, you can tell; you don't need to be told as much. This is why you sulk. Like most people, you want to be liked, Kate. You want to be included, and you're bad at hiding it.

I take your hand in mine. We walk and you perk up a little when Bob and one of his workers lead us to an open field. When we're settled with our ammo and our supplies, Bob gives the nod, and you are unaware of what happens next, of what is to come.

You watch as the door to the shelter across the way opens, your eyes peeled as it closes again. You look at me, and you raise your brow. You want to know what the holdup is. You aren't good at waiting, but I will teach you. Bob hands me ear protection, and I place it over your ears.

Then he takes you by surprise when he hands you the

rifle, and I swear you almost clap. You don't know gun safety, but you improvise.

You flinch a little. You're hesitant when Bob gives the signal, and the door opens. A man in an orange vest opens the door. Bob holds up his hand. You watch as the guy in the orange vest leads a man who is blindfolded out by the forearm. I see the hesitation in your stance. You watch, but you don't look to me for answers, and then a whistle is blown, and the blindfolded man takes off running.

"Fire whenever you're ready," Bob yells, and you do a double take. You don't ready your gun. You look at me instead, your eyes wild.

"This is Bob's version of hunting," I tell you, trying to steady you, trying to help you relax into my world.

The blindfolded man has gained a good two hundred yards toward freedom when I accept the fact that you aren't going to pull the trigger—that you aren't going to do it. I position my gun and take aim. I watch the guy fall in one fell swoop, and the shot rings so loud, it takes me a second to realize I've forgotten to place my own ear protection on and a second longer to know the shot came from your gun, not mine.

I look at you and then at Bob. You're grinning from ear to ear, and he is congratulating you on a nice shot.

"You didn't tell me we were hunting humans," you say, exasperated, and you're a little shocked, but you're happy too. Your hair's a mess, and I think I just fell in love.

"These aren't humans," Bob says correcting you. "These are war criminals." He smiles. "And there's plenty more where that one came from."

You swallow, your eyes grow wider, and you are buzzing. Another blindfolded man is brought out, and this time, it's Bob who goes in for the kill. You reach for my hand, and you squeeze, and you are a better shot than I imagined.

"Where'd you learn to shoot like that?" I ask you. You smile, and you look on as the second man falls and his blood spills out, pouring into the ground where the dry earth laps it up. Life giving life.

"Instinct," you tell me, eventually.

"Instinct... yes, of course," I say, and you shrug, and you are a natural, and this is how I know you are my forever.

❧

CHAPTER TEN

KATE

Amy is nowhere to be found. At least, not on this island. I know because I have looked here and there and everywhere and you have been of little help. You surprised me yesterday with 'human hunting' and I thought I knew you were the one before, but, if anything, this sealed the deal. You were right, this country is beautiful, and I feel so lucky to be here with you, even if I haven't found your ex-girlfriend. I will make it my life's work to extinguish her from this country, this planet, your heart, if that's what it takes.

You can tell that I'm unsettled, and you try, you really do. But it isn't helpful. I don't think you realize the source of my consternation has to do with the fact that you're still in love with another woman—but how can I let you in on this truth without making you think I'm crazy? I can't.

This morning, you told me you can only stay another day or two—max—and then you have to get back to work. Only when I asked what you're working on, you went silent. This is no way to have a relationship, Jude—if you won't open up to me, this can't last. We were scheduled to stay another week, and this is the way it starts? Already, you're letting your work get in the way. I can see that you're a workaholic, only that isn't an accurate description, is it? Your work is such a part of you that you don't know where one stops and the other begins. I saw this with my father, and it destroyed him, and it almost destroyed me. I won't let that happen to you, to us. Your work is who you are, I get it. But thankfully, now you have me to help you draw the line. In time, I will help you see there's more to life than making a living, and it will be the best gift you'll ever receive.

It's our last night here in Sri Lanka, and you insist on taking me down to the beach to watch the sunset even though we can see it clearly from our balcony, and I like being here, naked with you, I want to say. Still, you're insistent, and so I throw on a swimsuit and follow your lead.

When we arrive at the spot you've chosen, I can see why you made me come. You're very good at that, by the way. I tell you this even though I don't have to. It's the closest I can get to an apology for making you work so hard outside of bed. You deserve that much. I can see you've thought of everything here—that you've covered all the bases. You cover my eyes with your hand, and you lead me into the small cabana. Then you drop your hand, and it takes me just a second to register it all. It's dimly lit in here, and it's all set up with champagne and fruit, cheese, and other stuff, that we won't get around to eating. I know I shouldn't be, but I can't help but wonder if you did this for Amy too. You're trying to put me at ease, doing your best to show your love—to make me forget that you still want your ex, and I have to admit this isn't a bad way of going about it.

It's just that last night, I watched you sleep, I studied you, and I thought about us, about the future. You are the man I want to spend the rest of my life with, and did you know you sleep with one eye open, Jude? Well, you do. You don't trust me, this is clear, and you won't make killing you easy if that's ever the route I decide to take.

Not that I'm thinking of killing you—but falling in love is hard, and as I've mentioned, it's a long way down to the bottom. This is the happiest time of my life, being here with you, but it hurts some too. It hurts because of that thing nagging in the back of my mind. That thing has a name, and it's Amy. I have so much to say on the matter, but you're evasive. There's nothing quite like your first love, Jude, you know that. And I can't help but think what if she was to show up and take it all away? She could waltz in and snatch you up, and that's not a chance I'm willing to take. I won't gamble with my heart; I won't.

I know you would leave me in a heartbeat for Amy. This is why you told me about her in the first place. It was an offering, a warning not to get too close. I don't say this out of insecurity, either. I'm not an insecure person. I say it because I know that look, the one in your eye whenever her name comes up. I am a woman, and there are things women just know, and when your man is in love with someone else— well, that is one of those things.

Also, it's not fair, Jude—this game, it isn't a fair one. This makes it tainted, rigged. The rules are evidently tilted in your favor so long as your first love is out there hanging in the balance. And you're lucky not to know what that feels like. My first love is dead, and if you ask me, it's time we even the playing field.

~

THE CABANA CAUSES A HUGE FIGHT, AND ALL I DID WAS ASK IF you brought Amy here, and you lost it, Jude, you did. You're sexy when you're angry—but you're scary too. You grab me by the wrists and pin me to the daybed. You straddle me, and I hope I know what's coming next. But then I realize I don't because it isn't you, and it certainly isn't me.

It turns out, what comes next isn't remotely as good as what I was hoping for. Instead, you throw a massive fit. You tell me you tried to make this special, and I tell you that blowing up over a single question isn't special, and then you storm off.

After a few moments in which my world stops spinning, you waltz back in, and I think maybe I'll get lucky, that you'll get lucky too, but you only tell me you had a proposition for me, and then you thank me for ruining it. I tell you that you are not charming when you're being sarcastic, and you huff, and you puff, but you do not blow the house down. You simply walk back out.

I don't follow.

I, for one, plan to enjoy this cabana and my last night on the beach. I stare at the water for a long time, and I drink enough champagne to give me a slight buzz. Not a lot, but just enough to take the edge off, and I hope you'll wise up and see that you're overreacting. But you don't, and so I decide to go for a swim.

I meet Leslie in the water. She's avoiding something too. She tells me she likes the way the tide feels as it takes her over, and I know instantly that she'll help take my mind off you. She's here with her boyfriend. He's napping because he's old, she says, and sometimes we have to give a little. I like it when she says this. Maybe I should've given a little, and then I would be here with you and your proposition and not with someone going on and on about why I really should consider dating older men. She says she prefers doing so but warns that it comes with its own set of baggage. More so than the young ones—if you were to ask her. I didn't, and I don't know why she's telling me all of this, or why she can't see that I have my own problems.

But on the bright side, I guess it's nice to know I'm not alone. She wants to be friends, and we might have been had she not made such a fatal mistake. You should know that I didn't sleep with her, but I did invite her back to the cabana to share the remainder of the champagne. The truth is I wanted you to come back and find me there with a friend. I wanted you to know I can manage on my own, that I won't wait around. Then she kissed me, and well, I didn't exactly stop her. But if it's any consolation, it wasn't great. Also, she was drunk, and I don't like drunks.

We hung out for a bit, and then we went for a swim, but only one of us came back. She should have been nicer. She should have been a better kisser. She should have been a lot of things. But mostly, she shouldn't have said those things about you. She didn't know you. She didn't know us. She was wrong about all of it.

This is why I dunked her in the ocean and held her there until she stopped fighting. What other choice did I have, really? She wouldn't shut up, and I couldn't let her keep saying those things about love. I couldn't let her keep putting those ideas in my head. She was poisonous. I had to make it stop, and so I held her under, until finally she did, and then and only then did I feel better.

The thing is, sometimes you meet the wrong person at the wrong time, and that's what happened for Leslie. It is not what happened for us. We met at the perfect time, and she was wrong—all men are not assholes. Some men are just confused. You won't string me along forever the way she let those old men do to her. You won't leave me for another, younger version of myself, after we've built a life together. You won't. You and I, we had a misunderstanding, that's all. Not so different from Leslie and me. But then, look how that turned out for her.

～

CHAPTER ELEVEN

JUDE

We get to the checkout desk, and the lobby is insane. This place is teeming with people, and we're already late. This is your fault, obviously. I practically had to pull you out of bed, and trying to get you out the door was a whole situation in and of itself. I'm not used to this, this waiting game. If we don't hurry, we're going to miss our flight, and the line to the desk winds around the ropes twice. You look at me, and I look at you, and it seems there's a reason for the wait this time, unlike the shenanigans you pull. Apparently, a guest went missing last night. The man in front of us fills us in on the details, and I'm surprised that he's talking to us at all. Most people in here simply stare at their phones, and no one communicates anymore, and isn't that supposed to be the whole point of all of this standing around?

He tells us the woman had a fight with her boyfriend and that she said she was going for a swim but never came back. The boyfriend is in shock, he says. He caught a glimpse of him, and why people are always such voyeurs in times like these, I'll never know. He also heard the guy is complaining of chest pains, which I say means he's either overwhelmed or guilty. But you see things differently, and you surprise me too. You mention how sad it would be to have the last time you saw someone you loved turn out to be a fight. You squeeze my hand, silently telling me you're glad we made up, and I lean down and kiss your forehead, and I love that you're such a deep thinker.

When we finally reach the front desk, the checkout guy tells us to step aside, to hang tight, and eventually, a police officer shows up and ushers us over into a corner. Turns out, my name was on a cabana rental near where the woman was last seen, and immediately, alarm bells go off in my head. I look at you, and you shrug. I tell the officer that we were celebrating, and we don't recall seeing a woman, but then we were preoccupied, and you agree. You smile, and he buys it.

We turn to go, and then he pipes up, more out of curiosity than anything. "What were you two celebrating?" *Voyeurs, I swear.*

I grin and wrap my arm around your shoulder.

"Our engagement."

You don't miss a beat, and you smile in solidarity, and you pass the test. You are brilliant under pressure. Not many people get away without "tells" but you obviously aren't most people. I watched closely, and you showed none.

Not even when you lied to me indirectly.

You know more about that woman than you're letting on, and I can't help but wonder if you'll pass the truth test with me too.

In the cab on the way to the airport, you confess that you like my lie, and I don't tell you that I *actually* wasn't lying —that we should be celebrating right now, that we would be engaged if you hadn't brought up my ex-girlfriend in that cabana.

But that's water under the bridge now. Or at least, for our sake, I hope it is. Because in the warm afterglow of makeup sex, after you finally came back to me, ready to apologize, I asked that you never speak her name again, and you promised you'd try. I hate that word, try, Kate. Basically, it means you won't, and I'm "trying" to be patient about your lack of commitment causing our lack of commitment. But I'm not a patient man. You should know that. My ex-girlfriend, Amy, she forgot, and she didn't *try* and if you *must* know this is why I don't like talking about her.

You sense my irritation, and it seems to turn you on. You can't keep your hands off me, and I like this version of you. Your hand rests on my thigh, your fist around my heart. You wear passion like rich women wear pearls, ceaselessly, as though it's nothing. You act as though it's all the same. But it isn't the same, Kate. You're all over the place, and we have to harness this issue, we have to rein it in.

You're squeezing the life out of my heart. You're breathing air into my lungs. I'm drowning in you. And it seems you know a thing or two about that. But, then, I do too. You see, we are the same.

ON THE PLANE, I ASK YOU ABOUT THE WOMAN WHO WENT missing, and I hope you'll tell me the truth. You know what happened to her, and I want to know too.

"Tell me about last night," I say, and I watch your face. You don't seem surprised by my candor, and I wonder what does surprise you. Engagements on the beach, I'm guessing, and the grip you have on my heart tightens, and I hate you a little for ruining that for us.

"She said bad things about you. And then we went for a swim…" you offer, with a shrug. You are matter of fact about death, and I like that you're so open. I like that we speak in code.

"Kate, you can't go swimming with just anyone, you know. You didn't even know her," I say. You shoot me a look. I sound like your father, and yes, I mean what you think I mean.

"I knew her well enough," you reply, and your bottom lip juts out, and I could stare at you forever, and I will, you just have to let me.

"Yeah, well, still, you didn't think it through. Something bad could have happened…"

You smile and your face lights up. "It did."

I shake my head at your petulance, and we can't talk about this now, not here. You've made a mistake, Kate, and mistakes have to be rectified. You need to learn your lesson, and I look forward to teaching it, just as soon as this plane lands—just as soon as we don't have an audience.

In the meantime, you're smug, sitting there. You're pleased with yourself and killing does a body good. You're clearer than usual, happier, and I can see that you and I suffer the same affliction.

We love death.

Darkness pulses through our veins, it propels us forward, and we are seekers, always seeking. I casually lean over and ask you if you know the French call orgasms 'little deaths.' It's a message, and you and I we know the meaning of that better than most. We need the rush—of killing, of each other. We crave it, like nothing else. Except for this one thing—this thing I have now. This thing that is love—this thing that is you.

Killing and loving make us better, Kate.

But both have rules, and it's high time you learn what they are.

Being honest with me is at the top of that list.

~

THE FOLLOWING DAY, I DECIDE IT'S TIME YOU UNDERSTAND, and so I drive you out to a little spot I know that's not too far outside of town. I park beside the ramshackle old barn, and I tell you this is where I do my best thinking. I tell you that ages ago when it was a small thriving country store, my mother used to bring me here. She'd buy liquor. I'd get ice cream. There's no ice cream anymore, but that's okay because I have you.

You listen intently when I explain I have fond memories of those trips, of our little adventures, and this spot is often where I find myself when everything gets to be too much.

I tell you about one afternoon in particular. One I remember better than most. It was late summer and cloudy that day. The humidity in the air was almost unbearable, sweat pouring off of me as it trickled down my lower back. I think humidity does things to people. But that is not the point. That day, my mother asked me to come inside with her as she sometimes did, and in addition to her regular purchase—the latest gossip rag and a bottle of Jack—she placed a bottle of lighter fluid up on the counter.

When I asked her what it was for, as long as I live, I'll never forget the smile that lit her entire face as she explained she was going to teach me the art of building a fire. The flames will be brilliant, she said, and it will smell like revenge. On our way out, I asked what revenge meant because I was too young to know, but she didn't answer, not really. She simply clapped her hands and told me I'd see.

Later, back at home, once she'd finished her second drink

and I'd consumed my double-scooped ice cream cone, she ordered me into our Cadillac, which was odd because she usually didn't drive when she'd been drinking. "It's time you learn two things, son," she said, shaking her head as I climbed into the passenger seat. "It's time you learnt to drive, and it's high time you understood the sweet taste of revenge."

We drove to Sam Avery's house, or rather, I drove, sitting on her lap. She managed the gas pedal while I manned the steering wheel. "Look at the road, Mommy," I kept telling her, but she said I was doing a fine job, and mostly, she let her head lull backward against the headrest. She told me to tell her when to brake, and when to step on it, and I did my best to do a good job at that too. "Do you remember how to get to Sam's house?" she eventually asked, and it's a good thing I did because she hadn't given me any real direction.

I pause for effect, and I watch your expression. Then I go on, for you, for us. I explain that Sam was a man I knew only vaguely and only because he'd been hanging around the house recently since Dad had been away. My mom said he was fixing stuff around our place, and I figured he must have been doing a good job because nothing ever seemed broken.

When my mom and I finally pulled up in front of Sam's run-down ranch-style home, I wondered why he didn't spend more time fixing up his own house. I asked as much, and my mom laughed and told me I was the smartest boy in the whole world. Then she scooted me out of her lap and into the passenger seat. I watched as she took her handkerchief from her bosom, pushed in the cigarette lighter and then lit the material on fire. My eyes grew wider as she held the burning fabric out the window before opening the door. She stepped out and let the flames fall to her side. She stood there, thinking, or waiting, but only for a second. Then she made her way toward Sam's truck, all the while she kept the bottle of lighter fluid tucked close to her heart. The hankie was burning too fast, I wanted to call to her—it would burn her—she should be more careful. I had so much to say only my mouth was too dry, and so I looked on in utter amazement as my mother deftly and artfully poured the contents of the bottle over the truck. When she seemed satisfied with her work, she stepped back and tossed the burning handkerchief into the mix. She stood there watching with a look of amusement on her face as the truck went up in flames, slowly at first, and then all at once.

I thought we would stay and watch it burn all the way because it was really something to see. I don't think I'd ever seen a fire like that. Not before and not since. When my mom returned to the car, I asked if we could stay, but she shushed me and then ushered me into her lap. Then she put the car in gear and yelled at me to steer and said that some things are best left to the imagination.

Nonetheless, as we pulled away, I watched the fire in the rearview mirror, and later, once I couldn't see it any longer, I asked why she burned Mr. Avery's truck. "He lied," she said, her voice steady, in control.

"And some people, son, you just don't lie to."

"That's what revenge means?" I asked. "Not telling lies?"

"Revenge, Jude," she replied, "is punishment for messing with the wrong person."

"But how do you know?" I asked.

She laughed, and I could smell the liquor on her breath. "That's the beauty of it, son," she told me. "You don't."

∿

CHAPTER TWELVE

KATE

You drive me out to the middle of nowhere, and I swear you're going to kill me. The time has come for this to end, I feel it. I sense the change in you, and I bet people in normal relationships never worry about their partner killing them. That sense of security must be nice. But we aren't normal, you and I. To forget this, I realize, would be a mistake. Maybe it *already* has been a mistake. Maybe that's why we're here on this desolate farm to market road, quiet, distant, and so in love. Tell me, Jude, I want to say to you, was it? Was it all a mistake? But I bite my tongue.

I don't speak, and I stare at the sun. I know they say it's bad for you, but I do a lot of things that are. The light glistens off the dash; it dances, just like you and I, and it is blinding. I know too much about you, too much about your life. I've gotten too close, and now you're done with me, and well, we both know what happens to people who know too much.

You pull off the road, and you put the car in park, and it's scary—loving and fearing a person this much. That's not to say I'm afraid. I can handle myself. I just don't want it to end. I'm not ready for us to end, not like this. Not yet. You turn to me, and I wonder what's on your mind. I ask as much, I ask what we're doing here, and you surprise me with the most beautiful of stories. The way you tell it is a gift so beautiful that if it were to be the last to fall on my ears, well, I think I could live with that.

But I'd rather be alive instead, and so I settle in my seat, feel for the .35mm I have tucked into my waistband, and I ready myself for what comes next, ready myself to see what you're made of. But you stun me when instead of a gun you pull out a ring. My breath catches in my throat, and you don't kill me, but you do, when you ask me to spend the rest of my life with you, and maybe it's the same thing.

I consider your proposal for a second, and then I audibly exhale. You've saved me with your question, you've saved yourself. I tell you yes, of course, and you tell me you have a house all picked out in the suburbs. All it takes is a call to your real estate agent, you say, for it to be a done deal.

I wonder how I missed this when I was so sure it was over, only now you have it all figured out, and I feel like a minor detail, someone to fit into your best-laid plans, and this makes me both happy and sad. They say sociopaths can't feel, but the knot in the pit of my stomach is proof that they are wrong. You tell me you want us to work together, in your line of business. You think I'd be great at it, great at tracking people, but I'm not great. The most glaring example is the fact that I've yet to find Amy.

I don't tell you this because I've made a promise. Instead, I tell you I want nothing more. This is true, minus the knot, the one that's twisting, threatening me—threatening every-thing. It doesn't make any sense, but then I guess love rarely does. I'm supposed to be happy, and I am. I am so happy that I don't know how to just be. This is the thing about people like us—we're always on the run, always waiting for the other shoe to drop. This is a game we play, the killing and the planning—the hiding—we like to see how close we can get to the edge. You are my edge, Jude. You are the air I breathe, the knot in my stomach, the love of my life, and I don't know how to process something so wonderful being mine.

I stare at you, studying you, memorizing this moment, knowing I can't let it slip through my fingers—knowing I have to grab on and milk it for all it's worth, even if it kills me.

"So we're doing this," you say.

"Yes," I tell you. I smile as you slip the ring on my finger. I glance at it, and it's one I would have chosen myself, and maybe you do know me better than I think.

You laugh and say we'll get a dog, and someday, you say, we'll have kids. This is everything and nothing I've ever wanted being here with you. I don't know if you realize it, but our little pact, well, I might as well have just handed you my gun and pointed in my direction. You have the power to take me out. Only now, in more ways than one, and I'm not sure I trust you not to pull the trigger. I'm not sure I trust anyone—least of all myself.

"Kids," I say.

"A whole house full."

"Better start practicing now," I say, and then I climb over into your seat and press the button to slide it as far back as it will go. I lift my dress and press myself to you. I grind, contorting my body in ways that hurt so good, here, in this confined space. You kiss me, and it's deep. Your mouth is relentless, and soon, you are ready for more and so you undo your pants. You slide into me, your breath hot on my neck, and we move together—hurried and full of passion into the rest of our lives.

$\approx$

I'VE ALWAYS THOUGHT KILLING PEOPLE AND LIVING ON THE RUN were tough. But, turns out, those things pale in comparison to the reality of settling down. You know what's stressful? I'll tell you. It isn't choking the life out of someone. It isn't watching a person gasp for air or slipping peacefully off into a drug induced sleep—it isn't.

It's the details. It's wedding planning. Now—*that* is stressful. And don't even get me started on house hunting. This is supposed to be fun—but dear god, you have to choose just one, and how does one go about knowing which one that is? Houses are like people. They can be deceiving until you're all in—until you've settled in for the long haul—before you've gotten to know their bones.

I'm not sure it surprises you half as much as it surprises me—but I'm realizing that I haven't the first clue about anything in terms of domestic life. There are so many questions, Jude. So many variables. *Which neighborhood has the best schools? The best people? Where should we lay down roots?*

But it's the wedding that's tripping me up the most. There are so many expectations tied to weddings, whereas I have none. *Do we even need a wedding? Why not just elope?* You insist that we should have a ceremony, at the very least. You and your rituals. You want to show our future grandchildren photos, and you promise we'll regret it later if we take the easy route. I'm not so sure. I tell you people who have weddings are people who have friends and family, and you tell me not to worry. But I am worried. We don't need a ceremony, Jude—what we need are friends.

~

I WAKE UP COLD, SWEATY, AND PANICKED. YOU'RE ALREADY awake, watching me, and something feels very wrong. I can't breathe. You tell me to calm down. You take charge. You're ordering me to inhale slowly, exhale slowly. You countdown while I do, while I obey. You tell me to say your name, and I do.

I say your name over and over like my life depends on it, and it feels like it does. Eventually, my breathing settles, and when I'm calm, you ask how long I've had panic attacks.

I don't answer, but you squint your eyes, and you're all in, ready to fix this, ready to fix me. This is the first, actually— but I don't tell you that. Instead, I just shrug. "I get them sometimes when I'm stressed," I offer, sipping the water you've handed me. You're so prepared—you're always so prepared.

"What are you stressed about?" you ask, and I can't put my finger on it, but it's everything and nothing, and how do I begin to explain?

"Is it the wedding?" you want to know, and of course, it is. But I shake my head. The words, though, they refuse to be stifled. Suddenly, it seems they have a life all their own. I feel them as one by one they bubble up to the surface and spill out until the next thing I know, I am crying, and what is happening to me?

"It's just that we're going full steam ahead with this..." I sniffle, and you wait patiently, and I can't tell what you're thinking. This kills me, the not knowing. "It's just that—I feel like I don't even know anything about you..."

You furrow your brow, and I'm pretty sure I've caught you off guard. You weren't expecting this answer, and that makes it perfect. I don't understand how you can handle a girl who can't breathe like it's nothing, but when it comes to emotions, you're completely lost. You tilt your head. "What is it you want to know?"

"Everything," I tell you. "I want to know what made you, you..."

You nod slowly, breathing heavily through your nostrils.

They flare, and the muscles in your jaw twitch as you take it all in. I'm a mess, but you're good at handling messes, and you recover well.

"It's just that when your father called this morning... I realized I haven't even met him, and yet we're planning a life together—and I guess I just don't understand why I haven't met him."

I tell you this, and you listen. It all comes out hurriedly even though I've thought it through.

"You're emotional," you tell me, and I don't know what this has to do with meeting your dad, but I wait. "It's complicated," you finally say.

"So."

"So—my father is tough to nail down. He's busy. *We're* busy."

"He's retired, Jude."

"Yeah, but he fishes a lot."

"Fine," I relent. I cross my arms. "Tell me about him then."

I want details, and you give them. You tell me your father taught you everything you know—that despite the secrets your family held, you had a good childhood. For all of his shortcomings, you want me to know your father is a smart man, and even though you'll do it differently when it's your turn, you realize he did the best he could. It was different from the norm, growing up, you say, and we both know that being anything other than normal is tough. In your case, it meant you had few friends, and you were bored often. I want you to elaborate, and you do. Specifically, the times your Dad was between hunts, you admit. You say it changed the rhythm of your days when he was at home, that everything was sharper, more urgent, and more careful.

"How so?" I ask.

You purse your lips, and I watch your hands as you give

my question some thought. "Rudy wasn't happy unless he was hunting and—I find that I am much the same," you say.

You look away as you speak, and it's as though you've just revealed something to yourself, long forgotten. You look back at me. "I guess I've always assumed it came with the occupation—I assumed if one is wired for the high that comes with the thrill of the chase—then it makes it difficult to live any other way…"

"Yeah," I agree. "But what about your mom?"

"What about her?" you say, and you shrug. You know what about her, but I'm patient, and I don't press.

"Jean," you eventually sigh. "I already told you most of what there is to know about my mother…" you say, and you look away, and this is hard for you. "Jean was like most people. Not all good—and not all bad. She held Dad's secrets —but she always made sure to keep a few of her own."

"That must have been hard for you."

"It was." You meet my eye. "I learned early on that the more secrets Mom held, the more Dad liked to hunt…" you continue on, and I watch the muscles in your jaw twitch. This is your tell, and I wonder if you realize it. "Later," you say. "I came to understand that my mom's secrets were at least half of the reason he hunted."

"So your father is a killer?" I ask. I already know the answer.

You shake your head. "Not naturally—not like us."

I furrow my brow, silently urging you to go on.

"Rudy was a bounty hunter, mostly," you say, and you swallow. "Not that he was innocent, though—he killed on occasion… but only when he had to. Only when he had no other choice."

I nod slowly, and then I run my fingers down the length of your forearm. "What else?" I ask. I want to know more, and you are so much stronger than you realize. You can tell me. You just have to want to.

"Most people we knew thought my dad was a traveling salesman..." you tell me, and you laugh slightly, and I knew you could do it. I knew you'd let me in. "For a printing company..." you add. You shift. "I think they chalked his frequent absences up to going with the territory of that kind of career. But what they were forever trying to figure out was why we were so well off. Even back then, hunting people for money paid more than your average gig." You look me up and down and then you look away. "Not that we lived extravagantly or anything—Rudy hated anything flashy. But my mother, she thrived on it." You sigh. "But then, Jean thrived on a lot of things Dad didn't like." You meet my gaze. "Drinking was one of them... If Mom was between affairs and Dad was away—she liked to throw a few back. She couldn't help herself—anything, she'd tell me, to take her mind off the loneliness."

You go on, and your face is sad, and I wonder if you know how much I love you in this moment. "That was the thing about my mother—she always enjoyed a good party." You continue and then you exhale, and it's as though you've been holding this in for far too long. I watch your chest as you inhale, and you might as well be breathing for the first time.

That's the thing about me I think you don't quite realize. I'm gifted at reading people—maybe even more so than you are. I sense your pain. I feel it in my bones while you bury it, and they say I'm the crazy one.

"The problem was, though, when Jean drank—Jean liked to talk," you add, and you're still talking, and I have to say, getting in touch with your emotions looks good on you.

I tilt my head, considering how far you're willing to go, and you look away again. "This made keeping the secret that

Dad hunted people, sometimes killing them for a living, a bit difficult."

"That's where you came in."

"Yes," you say, meeting my gaze. "I learned how to clean up the mess they left behind." You exhale, and it goes on forever. "In the end, it turned out to be not *only* a great life skill—but a necessity in this profession."

"I can see that," I tell you, and then I snuggle up against your side. All of a sudden, I can breathe again. I'm satisfied, full on you, and the stories you tell. You wrap around me, and I know you won't sleep. But I will. I needed that. If I have to fake panic attacks to get what I need, then so be it, Jude. I guess you shouldn't be so good at cleaning up messes.

You're sitting over me the next morning, watching me, coffee in hand, and I don't think you ever sleep these days. I squint into the bright white light, and maybe I'm dreaming, or maybe I'm dead.

"Coffee," you offer, and it's too bright to see your face, which means I can't read your expression, but I'd confidently say there's a hard edge to your voice.

"Sure," I say, feeling for your hands. You place the cup in my hands, and the heat feels good against my lips. It eases the lump in my throat.

"The more I think about it..." you tell me, and you sigh. You're tired, and it shows. "The more I realize I should probably clear a few things up about my mother."

"Okay..." I say, and I sit up. Now that my eyes have adjusted, I study your expression. You look terrible.

You seem to read my mind, and you take the cup from me. I watch you take a sip, and I wait.

"Yes, she liked other men—yes, she was a serial cheater.

And sure—she turned to the bottle each and every time those affairs let her down… and often between—but she was more than that, too."

I swallow even though my mouth is dry again, and I don't think I've ever seen this side of you. I put my hand on your leg, and you stare into my eyes. There's something you're trying to say, and I'm having a hard time figuring out what that something is.

"It's important that you know she was the best mother a kid like me could have had," you say, and you inhale. You're on edge. "She was fun, and she was brilliant. And unfortunately, for a husband who was frequently gone—she also happened to be incredibly beautiful."

I never doubted that, looking at you. I almost say this, but then you let out a long sigh, and just when I think you aren't going to continue, you go on. "Jean was always the life of the party—the center of our little family. For a long time, it seemed the whole world revolved around her. And it did. But Jean taught me every bit as much about becoming the man— the assassin—I've become as my father did." You stand up and begin pacing the room. You run your fingers through your hair. "She taught me everything I know about people and what makes them tick. She taught me how to read them and how to play them."

"That makes you lucky," I say, and it sounds stupid, and it is. But I can't think of anything else.

"My father, on the other hand, he taught me the mechanics of how to hunt and kill. He drilled in the fundamentals about how to go about it without getting caught and schooled me on the business of getting paid well for it. But my mother—well, Jean, she taught me about fulfilling roles and putting on a show."

"I can see that," I tell you.

When you're finished saying what you need to say, you

come back to the bed, and you lay down beside me. You seem satisfied.

"Your mother… where is she now?"

"I don't know," you tell me, and you leave it at that. I don't press for more. You need sleep. You need a lot of things, Jude. Things I don't think you realize. You need closure on ex-girlfriends, and you need a mother. I don't know where either of them are—or how to fix you—or the fact that you don't sleep. But I can promise you one thing, I intend to find out.

CHAPTER THIRTEEN

JUDE

I 've given you everything. I've told you everything I know. Well, mostly everything. It's important to keep a little mystery in a relationship. My mother always said that. What I mean is—we're at the point in which we know we want to spend the rest of our lives together, but we're still on our toes, not too comfortable. After all, one should never get too comfortable. This is a good place to be, I think. But that doesn't mean it's not scary as hell. *'Til death do us part. Jesus.*

I'm feeling the gravity of such a commitment today, I have to admit. What no one tells you about relationships, and especially about marriage, is that death's the easy part. It's all the stuff in between that gets muddled up. I see this in couples all the time. They bicker over the most trivial of details—like where to go for dinner or who took out the garbage last—and it kills me, Kate. These absurd first world problems people use against each other, and I vow this will never be us. We won't be like that. We won't.

I know what I want, which means I know what I don't want. And I know I don't want another Amy. And I'll never again let a woman get too close. This I know for sure—I'll never again let one get ahold of me by the balls.

I'm irritated with you. In fact, after the shenanigans you pulled earlier this week, we aren't even speaking. You think I don't know what you're up to—but I do. You want things your way. And I don't think you want what I want at all. No, you want to argue over minutiae, insignificant details like flooring and granite and closet space. No one gives a fuck about closet space, Kate. If you can't keep your shit out in the open—chances are you don't need it.

You're spoiled, and you're wishy-washy, and quite frankly, I'm over it. So I took matters into my own hands and closed on a house. I hope you like it. I hope you'll be surprised—and isn't this what women want? A man who takes charge? Well, I took charge—so you'd better be thrilled when I take you there. Because the sad fact of the matter is, Kate, you can't make up your mind about anything, and I can't help but think you're dragging your feet has something to do with the fact that you're not sure about me. You're not all in, and you have to jump in with both feet—otherwise, this'll never work.

I try to convince you of this by divulging personal information—by telling you things I've never told anyone. Anyone except for Amy, that is. This method works magic, and for weeks afterward, you are on the upswing. Your moods are high, and you and I, we are blissfully happy.

But how quickly things with you change. You go from happy to moody faster than I can blink. That's why I bought you a house. Maybe you'll be happier if you don't have so much uncertainty—if you don't have an out.

Speaking of which, this afternoon, I picked you up from your apartment. You've been staying there for the past five days instead of at my place, and I don't like it. It's funny how soon you can get used to having a person around. Last week, you informed me you were 'PMSing' and you said you always needed space around 'that time of the month' and that you probably always will. Reluctantly, I gave it to you. But truth be told, I needed to get some work done. I need to close a few loopholes, and your apartment is one of them. Love and running don't mix. The same way as love and work don't mix. Your unhappiness pulls me away from that which needs my attention, and I have to work on that, and there is no balance where you are concerned.

I can't think, I can't eat. You consume me, and when we're not together, it only gets worse instead of better. This is what being in love feels like. I know because I've been in love before, but only once. Unlike the relationship you and I will have, that one was short lived, and so when you call and tell me you want to go to lunch, I see it for what it is. You miss me too, and no amount of bullshit hormonal upheaval can keep us apart. This is why I'm marrying you. This is why I closed on our future home without consulting you. Because none of that other stuff matters. I can't stay away, and now I know you can't either.

WE PULL INTO THE LONG CIRCULAR DRIVE, AND YOU ASK IF this is my father's place. You're dying to meet him, and you have no idea. I shake my head, park, and turn to you. I haven't stopped smiling since you climbed in the passenger seat. It is so good to see your face. I had no idea just how much I needed this, how much I need you, but now I do, and I won't let you run. Not anymore.

"Oh," you say staring at the house. Even sideways, I can see you're pale, and I don't think you're taking care of yourself. I don't know much about being a husband, I'll admit that. But I do know a husband is supposed to take care of his wife, and that's what I intend to do. So I did my research, and I realize what the menstrual cycle can do to a woman. I think you have vitamin deficiencies, Kate. You eat like crap, and I think it'll be good for you, having me around to set you straight.

"Well, whose is it then?" you pipe up, breaking my train of thought.

"Ours," I tell you, and I watch as your expression changes.

"What?" you say, and you glare at me. I nod toward the house answering without words, and you squeal, and when you look back at the three-story house, you gasp. "How can we afford this?" you ask. "It's massive."

"Do you like it?" I ask, evading your question with a question. You better, because it has a lot of fucking closet space. But I don't say this. I understand the value of letting things be.

You glance back at me, and you wiggle in your seat. Then you smile. "I don't know. I haven't even seen the inside." You're bullshitting, and you're glowing, and I know I made the right choice.

It makes me smile too, seeing you this happy, this surprised. I reach into my pocket and retrieve the set of keys. I hold them out, dangling them in front of you. "How about we fix that," I suggest, and you are grinning, and I'm pretty sure I've never seen you happier. But I will.

We're standing at our front door. Ours, Kate. I like the sound of that, and this is everything, I think, as I watch you unlock it. Once you have it open, you turn and look at me.

"Aren't' you supposed to carry me over the threshold?" you ask. You look at me, and you wait.

"Once we're married," I tell you, and you nod slightly because you know me, I like tradition.

"Yeah, it's best not to get ahead of ourselves," you chide. You like mocking me, and sometimes, I like it too.

There's more open space in here than you've ever seen, you comment, other than in the movies. Certainly more than you ever had growing up, even during your father's well-to-do years, you tell me. The kitchen, great room, and an office occupy the first floor, and I watch you walk through each of them. I stand back and let you have your space. I can see in your face you're plotting, you're imagining, you're planning, and I am too. Watching you here, I realize taking charge where you are concerned will always be the answer to everything, and I wonder if you realize it too.

You're here, and you're somewhere else, and you're running your fingers along the granite in the kitchen before you move on to the massive stone fireplace in the great room once more. It's like an episode of *House Hunters*, only you don't speak, and that show would be better if those people didn't either. I wonder if they know how superficial— how very *American*—they look, picking apart details like tile and window coverings, when people live in cardboard boxes, on the streets, under bridges. My guess is no. Thankfully, less fortunate people probably don't have giant screen TVs in order to see all their missing out on—so there is that.

"So I take it you like it then?" I ask eventually, needing to get out of my own head and into yours.

"It's... amazing," you tell me, standing at the back door. We have floor to ceiling windows, no window coverings yet, but I suspect you'll remedy that soon. You stand there for a while looking out at the backyard that isn't really a backyard at all. It's acreage, and you are right—it *is* amazing.

"*You're* amazing," I tell you, closing the gap between us. "I've missed you," I say, peering over your shoulder, and it's the truth. I won't let you keep running, Kate. I want you here with me—where you belong. I wonder what you're thinking, and you turn to me. You reach for my hand, and you take it in yours.

"It's so quiet here," you say. "Nothing like my apartment."

You have no idea. "You wanna see the other two floors?"

You smile, and I take that as a yes.

"Are you happy?" I ask, leading you upstairs.

"Very," you tell me, and it's all I wanted to hear. Simple, the way it should be.

I lead you straight into the master bedroom where you immediately walk to the center, standing in front of the California king-size bed.

'There's a bed," you tell me, stating the obvious, and I watch the way you move. You're elegant when you're surprised, and I like this side of you.

"Yes," I say, meeting you in the middle. We are fortunate, and we don't live under a bridge. We live here now, together. You put your arms around me, and you squeeze. Hard, as though you're thinking the same thing. Then I gently lay you backward onto the bed where we say so much without speaking at all.

WE'RE LYING NAKED ON THE ONLY PIECE OF FURNITURE IN THE place. I had it delivered to our new house specifically for this occasion. This is exactly as I pictured it, only better. I study the outline of you in the fading daylight, your breasts pointed toward the ceiling, your eyes pointed toward me. Your eyes bore into me, and I memorize your face. The sunlight filters through, and I swear I picked the perfect house, the perfect partner, the perfect bed.

It's almost too bad the light is fading fast, and soon, the room will grow dark, and I swear I want to know if it's possible to freeze time. "Stay here with me forever," I tell you, and you look up at me as though I'm magic, as though I've read your mind. A man could get used to being looked at like that, I tell you, and you smile.

"Do you think there are such things as accidents in this world?" you ask, and the beauty of your voice filling the empty room catches me off guard.

"Yes," I tell you, gently pinching your nipple.

You cup your breast, covering it, and then you swat my hand, and I love these games we play.

"I see," you say, and then you swallow. Your expression changes and I'm not sure I like this new version of you. You're lost somewhere in that head of yours, just like I was before we made love, but I am clear now, and I need to pull you out.

"What is it?" I ask. I don't like the look you're giving me, and I have to make it stop.

"There's something I need to tell you…" you say, and you bite your lip. You don't meet my eye when you say it, and a lump forms in my throat, and why must women insist on shock value? This day, this night, this life, it's supposed to be perfect, and you can't ruin it now. You can't.

"All right, spit it out," I manage.

You inhale, and then you let it out slowly. "I'm Mrs. Robinson…"

"Who?" I ask. I frown, and I don't follow.

"Your client," you say, studying my face, waiting for my reaction. "The one who hired *you* to find *me*."

""What?" I stutter. But you couldn't have known my client's name, and fuck, I wasn't expecting this curveball. I realize my mistake, but only partially. I should have asked better questions upfront. I should have seen this coming. But I didn't. Not in a million years. That's the thing my clients love about me. They say they want someone found, I find them. Unless it's a hit, I work on a need to know basis. This, though, I should have known.

"It just so turns out… that I wanted to find *you…*"

I tilt my head. "You did?"

"Yes," you say, and I feel the lump blocking my airway as it subsides a little.

"Why?" I ask, and you don't know it, I don't think, but this is everything I've ever wanted to hear. My head is spinning, and I like the feeling of the lump blocking my airway dissolving into nothingness. I swallow hard, and it is gone. I can breathe again and right here, in this moment, I have it all. Right here, it's clearer than it's ever been. You want me as much as I want you, and you always have.

You take a deep breath and tilt your pretty little head. You're mirroring, either knowingly or unknowingly, but either way, I like it. "I wanted something different… I wanted something that would last forever…" you say, and you have found it, and I am over the moon.

"What do you mean by that?" I ask, and I want to hear you say it.

"I guess I just wanted to find someone who holds the same secrets I do. I wanted someone who suffers the same affliction. You and I, we hunt, Jude. We take what is ours, and we don't leave things to chance. Especially not important things… like finding a life partner…."

"Then why did you go on those dates upfront? Why'd you join those dating sites?

"It was all a diversion…really," you tell me as you flick your hair to the other side. "I had to work you. You're the kind of man who needs winning over," you say, and you are right. I am. "But—I liked that you weren't easy… I mean who wants that?" you tell me and you sigh. "And if you haven't noticed…the others—well, they're all dead…"

All of them? Surely not. You don't work that fast. Do you?

"Right," I say, avoiding and evading. It doesn't matter anyway. You are brilliant.

"This is how I know we'll be together forever," you whisper, and you grin. "You know my secrets, and I know yours..."

You don't know them all. You don't know about Amy, I think. What would you say if I told you? Would you still love me if you knew what I'm capable of?

"I'm impressed," I admit, biting back the questions that swirl in my head. "I have to say, you're even better than I gave you credit for..."

You furrow your brow, and then you do a double take. "So you're not angry?"

"Angry?" I say.

You squint, and you fold your lips. You were expecting a different reaction. But I won't give you one. Not now.

I shake my head. "Nope. Not a bit."

You smile. But I don't think you're buying it. "And why is that?"

"Because I'm glad you found me... Because I wanted this. I've wanted it for a long time. Ever since—" I say, and you glare at me.

"Ever since what?" you ask.

"Ever since I first laid eyes on you," I tell you, and I improvise. Then I motion toward the space between us. "And now I have it...and it feels like I've been looking for you longer than I ever realized."

"Really?" you ask, and I pray you leave it at that—that you let it go.

"Of course... it's not that I didn't want someone to share my life with... I just never figured it was possible. I mean... I'm not exactly conventional. And as they say—you don't miss what you don't have. But then you came barreling into my life, and that was that, and I can't imagine having to miss this."

You stick out your bottom lip. You're impressed with my answer. "So I guess that settles it then?"

"Settles what?" I ask.

You laugh, and when you recover, you lower your voice. You speak in hushed tones, and I'm not sure why because it's just us. "You thought you were trapping me… in your line of work, I mean," you tell me, and you smile, and you like winning, so I let you. "You thought you were going to turn me in and make a buck off of me—" you add and then you wink, and I want to eat you up. "And all the while I was trapping you right back."

"Yes," I say. "We're trapped. Together."

You glance around the expansive room. "This isn't a bad place to be trapped," you comment.

"No, it isn't," I agree, but I don't take my eyes off you.

When you meet my gaze, your eyes narrow. I watch as you suck in a deep breath. You hold it. "There's something else," you eventually say. You sit up. I wait, and I hold my breath too.

"I'm pregnant," you tell me.

You're what? I want to ask, but the words won't come.

You laugh, but just barely. "I know. It's *so* soon."

"Wow," I say, and it's all I can manage. The whole world and everything in it spins in slow motion. We both stare out the window. Eventually, you lay back down.

"Are you happy?" you ask, reaching for my hand. The room has turned dark, and I can't see your face, but I sense what you're feeling. I'm feeling it too.

"I've never been happier," I tell you, and it's the truth.

"This house won't be this empty for long. It won't always be this quiet," you say, and you are right. There is so much work to do. Wow. I'm going to be a father. I am in love with you, something I once thought was impossible—after everything, after Amy.

I never thought I wanted a family, Kate. I never wanted this, not really. Family life doesn't suit this line of work and domestic life always seemed a bit out of reach for a killer like me. It seemed impossible that I could have it all—work I love, a woman who loves me, and now a child. And who knows? Maybe it still is. Maybe we live in a glass house, and it'll all come crashing down. Maybe happiness like this can't last. But in this moment, lying here with you, I believe anything—even the impossible might be possible.

THREE WEEKS LATER, WE'RE ALL MOVED IN, AND I TURN IN THE keys to your apartment. You've been too tired and too sick to really do much of anything moving related, but I tell you what, you sure can order furniture and organize workers like a boss. You have all of these ideas, and I swear it's like you're already nesting. And I know all about nesting. I've read the books. I've done my research, which is why I don't think you've completely lost your mind when you tell me we need to dig up a quarter of an acre of our backyard so that we can grow our own food. This new version of you, she is interesting, Kate. I'll give you that.

I have to leave town for work, and you know how much I hate leaving you. I ask you to come, but you say there's still so much to do around here that you can't imagine leaving now, and it's like you're an expert at guilt.

This leads to our biggest fight yet. I buy you a parting gift in the form of a dog. Roscoe is a well-trained guard dog, a German Shepherd, which I paid thousands for. You need Roscoe, Kate. You need protection. But mostly, you need practice caring for something other than yourself. I leave that part out, and you still don't take kindly to my gift. And he knows. Animals sense these kinds of things. I tell you this, but you don't care, and there's a part of me that wonders how you'll be as a mother. I tell you this too, and that's when I see just how crazy your crazy can be. What can I say—I guess we're both learning.

The second argument comes just as soon as I step off the plane after I've reached my destination. I switch my phone off airplane mode, and as I check it, I panic when I see I've missed thirteen of your calls. You're not the kind of woman to call more than once, and so this can only mean one thing. Something's wrong. I try you back, but you aren't answering my calls, and I'm so sick with worry that I can't breathe, and I postpone my meeting. A meeting, I might add, that I've flown halfway around the world for. Not to mention, I'm meeting with people who do not understand the postponement of anything. These are high-profile people who are paying me a lot of money to do what I'm told. I knew I shouldn't have come.

Short of hopping back on a plane and flying home, which I am tempted to do, eventually, I do the only other thing I can think of and call that redheaded neighbor girl who came 'round with homemade cookies the day the mover's arrived. You snuffed your nose at her and refused to eat them saying they were probably laced with poison. You're so moody these days. But I thought she looked nice. Luckily, I am right, she *is* nice because she left a card with her phone number on it in case of an emergency, and when you call me more than a dozen times and then don't answer your phone afterward— well, Kate, I call that an emergency.

You apparently do not agree—because when you finally return my calls, you're screaming about the redhead, and the dog, and how you killed the gardener after he tried to stiff us. You're yelling in my ear about burying him in the backyard, and 'my damn dog' digging him up, and this is why you were calling? I let you finish, and then I hiss into the phone that you shouldn't be killing people anyway, and what were you thinking? You're pregnant. I want all the details, I want to know how you did it, and *exactly* why, but we've already said too much, and surely the NSA is listening in on this one. I mention the 'N word'—no not that one, geez, I'm not that bad a person—I'm referring to the one that clues you into the fact that we likely have an audience. But you don't take the hint, and I probably could have said anything, and so you keep going. You're irritated. You want to know why I rung the nosiest neighbor possible. You want me to know that she almost caught you re-burying the gardener. You tell me I don't understand anything, and I tell you that leaving a voicemail could have avoided all of this. Then you hang up in my ear right when I was about to ask why we can't just have normal people problems.

CHAPTER FOURTEEN

KATE

This isn't good, I think, dropping my shovel. It hits the ground with a thud, and I have to will my eyes not to follow because if they do the girl's eyes will too.

"Your husband called," she says, and she squints because of the afternoon sun and maybe the weather gods are on my side.

I quickly realize the blinding sun is not enough and through labored breath, I begin panting. "My inhaler," I huff, and I point toward the house. I watch as she looks around, she's confused, and so I turn up the heat. I suck in and hold my breath until I can feel myself turning blue. The girl panics and it's a good thing. I wasn't really in danger because let me tell you, she needs to be the last person you call next time. This one clearly isn't very bright. Thank god for small favors.

"In the kitchen, in the drawer," I mouth. I watch as she goes toward the house, and then I bend over and place my hand on my knees.

I give her a thirty-second head start and then I follow. I'm limping like one of those characters on the *Walking Dead*, and I think my acting is on par, which isn't saying much. When I reach the kitchen, I find her rummaging through drawers, and it does feel like we're living inside that show. And I'll play the calm one, I think, as I turn on the faucet and fill a glass of water. I down it, and then I search the backyard for a sign of anything remiss. Luckily, with the exception of his hand, which I'd kicked on my way in, I'm pleased to see the rest of his body is in the hole, hidden from our current vantage point.

"Thank goodness you're here," I say once I've fake-caught my breath. "Kate," I add, extending my hand.

She looks at my dirty hand, and she smiles. "I know," she says. "I'm Josie," she adds. "We met the first day you moved in."

"Right," I say, washing up.

"Your husband called. He is worried about you," she tells me, and I swear there's a hint of disapproval in her voice. "I told him I'd check in on you, and then when I saw the work truck out front, well, I figured I'd better come over right away. You know... you can never be too careful. Especially when you're dealing with contractors. There are some real crazies out there... Craigslist killers, you hear about a new one every day it seems like," she exclaims, hurriedly and then her eyes grow wide. "Did you hear about that murder down near campus? So random... such a shame. And then there was—"

"No," I say cutting her off. I've had enough. "I don't follow the news."

"Oh," she says as though it's my loss. I can tell she's one of those perpetually happy people that nothing bad has ever happened to, and she looks so young standing here, so concerned about me receiving play by play information of all the evil this world has to offer that I hope for her sake she stays that way.

"The guy's truck broke down. That's why it's still here.

Needless to say, he didn't finish the job. Which is why I was out there," I tell her and almost point. I'm slipping. I have to be smart, and maybe I need a nap. "I guess I didn't hear my cell all the way in here."

"Hmm," she says under her breath, and that's when I see your damned dog. He has the gardener by the shirt, and he's tugging him out of the hole, and I thought I locked him up, only to find out he's not a regular dog. Of course, you couldn't just bring home one of those, you bring home a monster, fucking Houdini, an escape artist at the most inopportune time.

"Oh my god," I screech grabbing Josie by the hand. "I almost forgot," I say, leading her through the great room, toward the front door. "I have to be somewhere. I'm sorry. I hope you'll forgive me," I add, practically pushing her out the front door. "I hate being rude."

"No worries," she calls out as the door shuts in her face. "I'm just glad you're ok," she adds through the closed door. Her voice is too chipper for someone who has just had a door slammed in their face, and I shake my head. I'll have to remind her about trespassing and your vicious dog. It seems like the kind of story she'd like, I think, listening for her to retreat. Maybe that will be enough to keep her away, but probably not. When I see that she's finally gone, I turn and press my back to the door and sink to the floor. *What have you done, Jude?* What have you done?

I AM LITERALLY KNEE DEEP IN A HOLE TRYING TO BURY THE GUY who stole money from us when our redheaded neighbor girl shows up all stealth like. It isn't pretty the way she sneaks up on me like a freckled little ninja, and for a moment, I am afraid I am going to have to bury her too.

Three tries, that's how many I gave that man to do the right thing. Instead, he tore up our lawn and refused to fix it. In the process, he broke the sprinkler system, and then he lied about it. It mattered not that I showed him the security footage. He still denied it. You have this place outfitted like a prison, no move goes unnoticed, and I have to say, it comes in handy at times like these.

It took six phone calls to get him back out here, and a letter from an attorney who doesn't exist. When he finally showed up, I watched as he fixed the lawn, and I offered him lemonade laced with horse tranquilizers. It was a hot day. Needless to say, he drank a lot of lemonade. When he finally passed out, I used one of your belts to strangle him. He barely fought, and by barely, I mean not at all. Maybe I overdid the tranquilizers. It's too bad, I like a little bit of a fight. But he was a big guy, and I'm pregnant, and so I'd rather have given too much than not enough. Oh, and the belt, it's your favorite. I'm sorry about that.

Or rather, I was just a tad until I realized you called the redheaded ninja over here to check up on me. She almost busted me, Jude. She surely would've had I not feigned nausea. I mean, the guy's hand was practically hanging out of the hole when I realized she'd made it through the gate. I had to step on his rubbery, purple, tie-dyed fingers in hopes that she wouldn't see. My feet aren't even that big. It was a disaster, and I'm not sure you'll ever understand. Let me paint you a picture. It's important you know how close we came. How close I came to having to kill her. Then we would have had to move, and to tell the truth, I like this house.

Which is precisely what I was thinking when I looked up and saw her standing there.

You really should be more careful.

～

YOU RETURN FROM YOUR TRIP, AND WE FIGHT FOR HOURS, AND then we make up. You grill me about the gardener. You grill me about the neighbor girl, and you want to know everything. When I tell you I called a tow truck for the gardener's vehicle, you tell me this was a mistake and according to you, everything I do is wrong. You and Roscoe dig up his body, and then you pull into the garage where you've placed his corpse. I watch as you load it up in your trunk, I study the plastic you use, and you've thought of everything. Maybe next time, I'll do it your way. But probably not. I don't know where you're taking him, but you say he can't stay here. I like the idea of rotting flesh fertilizing my flower beds—but you say no, that's crazy. I tell you roses laced with revenge smell the best, and you don't laugh. You tell me we'll just buy the regular mulch stuff.

When you get back from your disposal mission, I almost ask where you've taken him. But I bite my tongue instead. I hate it when you shut me out, but we still aren't speaking. Apparently.

The following morning, you wander around the house, going from room to room. You're up to something. I just haven't figured out what.

You bring me coffee, and you instruct me to get dressed. When I don't budge, you tell me we're going to see your father. You say it's time the two of us meet. That way, if you're out of town, and I get myself in trouble again, you'll have someone to call. I tell you I'm capable of handling things just fine, and you snort while silently I plot your murder.

I'm still considering how I'd do it as I throw on jeans and a sweater. It's a good thing you've taught me all about disposal. I was just going to go with the garden. You think your shit doesn't stink, so you'd probably make great fertilizer.

You watch me dress, and I ask if he's expecting us. I get the feeling he isn't, and you utilize your usual evasion tactics by telling me you know your father, and you know where to find him. He's on the boat every morning at 8:00 AM, rain or shine, you offer, and I take it this means I'm right.

We head out, and I'm surprised to see it's raining. It's the kind of fine mist that promises of more to come, and there's the slightest hint of a chill in the air, and I think maybe fall might just arrive after all. This explains at least half of the reason all I want to do is stay in bed, and I don't remember a time I've ever been so tired.

On the drive out, I'm sick a few times, and you have to pull over, but it's ok because you tell me you've planned for this, and you try not to let the stench of my vomit bother you. I start to mention you just had a dead body in here, but you don't seem to be in the mood, and so I stare at the rain, instead. You do your best to focus on the task at hand. You tell me this is important, but I already know because you've mentioned no fewer than three times how imperative it is that we get to the dock by eight.

I stay quiet after this, and you think something is bothering me. It would be an educated guess, but I'm too tired to fight. Mainly, it's that my insides sway, and my stomach feels like there's an ocean inside and the tide is going out and coming back in. I count silently as it goes in and out and in again, and the motion is occurring too fast for my brain to catch up.

I'm not sure which way is up and which is down, and I want anything other than to be in this car headed toward a boat of all things.

You ask if you should turn around, and I tell you no. The only thing I want more than to be out of this car is to meet your father, our child's grandfather. I need to know that this baby will be ok—genetically speaking. I need to see where half of his or her genetics originated. This thinking is a bit backward I realize now. First things should come first. But what can I do?

I've already told you no fewer than nine times that everything is okay when you ask again. I tell you I am fine, and you say you hate that word, *fine.* You tell me this is something we're going to have to work out, and I tell you being pregnant is harder than I thought. Maybe you'll draw up a contract, you tell me, and I cringe because you are serious. I consider ten ways to kill you in that moment, and you really have no idea. I know because you're going on and on about some stupid nonexistent contract, and you think you're funny. In it, you say, you'll include all the rules for marriage, and they will be different than most couples, and we'll keep a list of words we promise to never say. Fine, you assure me, will be at the top of that list.

I tell you that everything is still 'fine' when we arrive. And for the most part, it is. The waves of nausea have subsided just a little and the fog in my head has lifted. This is when I realize I haven't actually thought this through. "I can't go on a boat," I tell you. "I'm pregnant."

But, like most things, you've prepared for this too. You shake your head, place your hand on my forearm, and offer a sly smirk. I want to hit you and wipe it right off. You wave me away.

"I've checked the rules, and it's fine," you say. You make sure to emphasize the word *fine,* and it's in this very moment the whole world and everything in it halts, and I realize that despite your inherent arrogance, what a great father you are going to make. Unlike me, you're detail oriented, and obviously, this drives me mad on occasion, particularly now, but in reality, I realize we are going to desperately need this quality if we're going to succeed as parents. It's shocking, I don't understand how I can go from hating you to adoring you in two seconds flat, but this must be what they mean when they describe pregnancy hormones.

I almost tell you this, but you pinch the bridge of your nose, and you sigh. "We have to go," you order, reaching for the door. "We're meeting my father," you remind me as though I'd forgotten. "And he's very punctual."

"Why didn't you just say so?" I ask, climbing out of the car. It's my best attempt at sarcasm and still, you miss the point. I know because you tilt your head and study me for a moment, and then you force a smile and tell me you don't understand women at all.

YOUR FATHER LOOKS DIFFERENT THAN I IMAGINED. FOR starters, he's a lot shorter than you are and rougher. You must look like your mother. Being here is good, I think, despite the fact that I hate boats. But it's clear from the moment we step foot on the boat that your old man wasn't expecting us. His posture is defensive, and it takes him a moment to relax once he realizes who we are. You introduce me, and he isn't welcoming—although he isn't exactly rude, either.

At any rate, I understand instinctively that I need to hold back. I don't extend my hand. I want your father to think I'm as ambivalent as he is, even though I'm not. I don't need to win him over, and I don't know why we're here today, in this shitty weather, and I don't care aside from the fact that I'm curious to learn about the man who is my unborn child's grandfather. I wonder if you've told him about the baby.

"Women and boats don't mix, Jude," he says, and you look at me. "I figured you were smart enough to know that," he adds, answering my question as though he'd read my mind.

His eyes are as clear blue as the water, and I wonder if the baby will have eyes like his or brown ones like yours.

"No worries, Pops," you offer. You smile, but it's strained. "We aren't planning on going out with you. You know me... I've never been one for fishing. But I did bring donuts... and Kate."

"Lydia," he counters. "You mean you brought Lydia."

"Right," you say, and you look over at me again and instantly, I hate the both of you. You should have warned me about what I was walking into. You should have told me what I was up against here—how much your father knows about me. "Anyhow," you say looking back at your father, "she goes by Kate now, Pops, and she's helping me on the Hathaway case, and I thought you might want to check her out... maybe offer some tips," you continue, and you've solid-ified the two of us as a team. I can't help but smile. You've just clarified my position in your life, and maybe I can forgive you for ambushing me.

We talk a bit more, or mostly you talk, about fishing and the weather, until you get a call. You glance at your phone, and you tell me you have to take it. My eyes follow you as you step down into the cabin. Your father, he wastes no time. He sighs loudly, and he readies his line and I know nothing about this kind of fishing.

"Kate," he says and I'm certain he's telepathic. "You ever do any fishing?"

I tell him I haven't, and he says this is good. He says that inexperience can make a person blind to what should be obvious, and I don't understand where he's going with this or how what he's saying is in reference to anything good.

"Hmmm," I say. "I don't know... I think experience is pretty important."

"No," he counters. "*Learning* is important."

"True," I agree.

"Do you know what the best way to learn is?" he asks, and he meets my gaze.

"Yes," I tell him, and I realize where this is going. "You have to get your hands dirty."

"Ah," he says, tossing out his line. I study him as he pulls it back in and then shakes his head. "But you're leaving out the most important point."

"I am?" I ask. I play dumb. I give him what he wants.

"Yes." He smiles, but it isn't genuine. "The best way to learn anything is by making mistakes."

"Huh," I offer, and I consider his sentiment. Then I furrow my brow, and I ready my ace. I sigh. "Then I guess you should've learned your lesson by now."

"What lesson would that be? Trust me, I've learned many…" he tells me, but I can see that he isn't surprised by my refusal to agree with him.

"The one about lying to Jude…"

He cocks his head, and I take aim. I don't know how I know, but I know. "You aren't Jude's real father," I say.

His face falls. "I beg your pardon."

"You see, Rudy," I tell him, and I sit up straighter in my seat. "Can I call you Rudy?" I ask before I tilt my head. I wait.

He shrugs. "By all means."

I sit up just a little straighter, and then I search his eyes and realize this is how I know.

"What color eyes does Jude's mother have," I press.

He winces, and he knows I'm onto him. "She had blue eyes…" he says eventually, and suddenly, he seems far off.

"Had?" I ask.

He looks at me but doesn't answer, and I wonder what else he isn't saying. "The thing is…" I sigh. "When you're a novice at all of this relationship stuff… you get to know a person. I mean, *really* get to know them, if you know what I mean—" I pause, but I don't give him a chance to respond.

"And when you know someone as well as I know Jude, well then, you know who they are...which means, you also know who they aren't."

"Is that so?" he asks, and he shifts and then we listen as you climb the steps. You hesitate at the top stair, and you look from me to your father and back. "Sorry about that," you apologize. "But work is work," you say, smiling at Rudy. Then you look at me and furrow your brow. "So, what did I miss... what were you guys talking about up here?"

I smile, and I stand. I give Rudy a chance to answer, and when I realize he isn't going to, I sigh. "Oh, you know," I say, waving my hand in the air. "Just more of the same... fishing and the weather and all of our deepest, darkest secrets..."

You laugh. "I'm sure."

Rudy checks his watch. He purses his lips.

"We'd better go," you say, and you reach for my hand. I let you take it in yours, and we are one.

Rudy stands too. He extends his hand in my direction. It's a peace offering. "It was a pleasure to meet you, Kate," he tells me. His smile is forced, and he leaves little doubt that he wants us off his boat.

To make a point, I offer the hand you aren't holding even though it isn't the appropriate hand to shake with. I slip my hand into his. His hands are warm, his handshake is firm, and you know what they say—*warm hands, cold heart.*

"Hopefully, you'll come back soon," he tells me, and I nod and for the briefest of moments, the three of us stand there, hand in hand, bonded by our secrets.

CHAPTER FIFTEEN

JUDE

One sunny afternoon, a few weeks before the wedding, we're lying on the couch, your head in my lap. The incident with the gardener is now a mere memory, one for the most part, we've put behind us. You seem to have accepted the notion that we have to be more careful here, now that we've settled in suburbia. It was a bitter pill to swallow for you, but choke it down you did, the knowledge that you can't kill anytime things don't go your way—you can't murder someone anytime it strikes your fancy. I'm hopeful that I've sold you on the idea that we have to be meticulous about our kills here—otherwise, we'll have to run, and then we'll always be running.

Also, you're feeling too bad these days for your old shenanigans anyway. In fact, you haven't moved in hours it seems. I'm starting to worry again that you might not, and so I lightly touch your hair.

"Jude," you whisper, and I wait for you to say more. Your head is in my lap, and when you don't speak up, I assume you're talking in your sleep. You do that from time to time. You've been sick for two days straight and again all morning, and I canceled my work trip when we had to make an emergency run to the ER where they determined you were dehydrated, and I was sick with worry. I didn't like all the poking and prodding they did, all of the useless questions they asked. All I wanted was for them to fix you.

You're still not yourself, but at least you're home where I can take care of you. They gave you fluids, and you seemed to perk up, but now I'm wondering if it truly did any good.

At least some good did come out of it, though. They asked if we wanted to take a peek at the baby and before we knew it, there 'it' was—a black and white blob flashing up on the screen. We watched the heartbeat swish and thrum, and I swear, Kate, it was the first time I truly felt what it means to be alive.

"Jude," you say again, and I realize you weren't dreaming.

I lean down, bending, doubling over to meet your gaze. Upside down, I study your expression. Your face is troubled. "I was just thinking… what if you'd gone…on your trip…I would have had to call a taxi to take me to the hospital… or an ambulance…"

"But I stayed."

You swallow, and you need water. "I know… it's just… well, now that it's not just the two of us any longer… I think it's probably time we make some friends. You know, just in case."

I do know. But I don't say this. I see the concern on your face, and I lean my head back against the couch so you won't see my face. I won't add to your anxiety over the 'what ifs' because I understand what you're feeling all too well. Seeing the baby this morning made everything more real. It's different now, and you're feeling it too. Of course, you are.

"There's always the neighbor girl," I offer.

You sigh. "I know. I've been thinking that I need to go

over there and thank her..." you sigh. "Whenever I'm feeling better."

"I think that's a good idea."

You scoot closer toward me, and then you inch away. "We don't have any family, Jude."

"We have each other."

"Yeah, but what about if something happens to one of us... what then? Or both?"

"There's Rudy."

"Right," you scoff. "It's not like he really wants to be involved."

"We'll figure it out, Kate," I tell you, stroking your hair. I made a move to get up, but then I decide against it. "Are you hungry?"

"God, no."

"But the medicine, it is helping, right?"

You're pale, and I can tell you aren't well, and I wonder how long this can last, how long before we can go back to normal. "I haven't thrown up..." you say, and there's that, but I can't help but worry this will be the new norm.

"You need water," I advise. You agree without speaking, I see it in your eyes, and I reposition you so I can scoot out from beneath you.

"When I was a little girl, sometimes when I'd get locked in my room, I would pretend I had a different mother and a different father. Sometimes I'd make up a whole family, and I swear, Jude, there were times when it almost felt real."

You catch me off guard with your words. This isn't like you, to talk about your past, and I decide not to make a move for the kitchen just yet. I let you settle back in. "Tell me about them. About this fake family—"

"Well, my mother's name was Harriett, and she looked just like me, only older. My father was Tom, and he was tall and strong, and he liked to read the newspaper. That's what I remember most about him. He was always telling me about stories he'd read." You strain to see my face. I can tell you're trying to gauge my reaction, but I won't give you one. Quite frankly, I don't know what to think about this softer, frailer, version of you, but I do know that I'm interested in hearing more, and so I raise my brow willing you to go on.

"I had a little sister, Lucy. She was sweet, and she looked up to me. I kept her out of trouble mostly." You stretch, and you exhale. "I can still picture them now, just the same as always. Isn't that weird?"

"I don't think so…"

"What about you? Did you ever wish for a different family?"

"No," I say. "There are things you hope for, and there are things that hurt to touch. For me, that was one of them."

I watch your face fall, and then you turn over and roll into me. You bury your head against my stomach, and you cry, and I don't know if it's the hormones or something I said. Maybe it's a little of both, and you see, that's the thing about hope, Kate. It's a dangerous thing.

FOUR WEEKS LATER, WE RECITE OUR VOWS BY THE LIGHT OF A thousand lanterns, in a sculpture garden, under a full moon surrounded by beautiful things that take their time and seldom last.

You wear cream-colored lace, a dress that so delicately touches all the things I love about you. You say it's vintage, and you look so beautiful that I forget the rest. I don a tux, specifically purchased for this occasion because I prefer fresh starts while you like things with history.

Your face is glowing as you walk down the aisle toward me, a little with surprise, but mostly, I hope, with love. You said we needed friends, and I surprise you by inviting the entirety of our neighborhood. I don't like a show, but this deserves as much, and mostly, I just want the best for you.

"Who are all of these people," you ask later after we've said our 'I do's' once the wedding planner has whisked us off for photos.

"Our neighbors," I say, and I can't take my eyes off you.

"Hmmm," you murmur and a camera flashes.

"There's more."

"Oh?" you say, and it's a question but your tone is sardonic, and I've always enjoyed you like this.

"Remember that family you told me you wanted?"

You nod so slowly it almost doesn't count.

"Well, I found them."

"What?" You glare at me incredulously, and then you double over laughing. I wonder if it's too much. But I suspect it isn't.

"They're actors," I whisper in your ear as the photographer ushers us to a second location "But our guests won't know that."

"This is crazy," you say, and I smile.

"I know," I tell you, and you lean in closer so she can get the shot, and so long as I live, I'll never forget the way you look at me in this moment. I take you in my arms and instinctively, I place my hand over our "honeymoon baby." And there we are smiling for the camera, sharing secrets— two people with history, making a fresh start.

We honeymoon in Mexico. It is actually a working trip for me, the one I canceled before the wedding when you got sick. But, of course, I don't tell you this. I don't want to ruin a good thing over a hit. You're still a little shaky, which is the only reason I considered combining the two. I know you need your rest, and this will give me a bit of free time to take care of the hit.

The Zofran the ER doc prescribed for the nausea is helping, but I wish it helped with your mood. You swing high, and you swing low, and I never know what's coming.

Mostly, we just stay in bed. I don't tell you about the hit, and I don't tell you that I'm considering hiring a caregiver for you. Not just so I can keep tabs on you, but also because I can't be there all the time. You need someone who can take care of you when I'm not around. I'm dreading this conversation, but it can't wait forever. For now, though, I need to focus. For now, we need to be happy.

The night before we're set to leave, I leave you in our room sleeping while I meet my contact to retrieve the weapon I'm to use and to get specifics on the mark. My hit is here vacationing with his mistress, which serves as a minor complication, but not one, I decide, that can't be handled.

I spot the two of them in the disco, and I watch them as I fake sip a margarita. I consider going back to check on you just in case you've woken up, but you seem to sleep so soundly these days, I think better of taking the risk of waking you just for the sake of being sure. This turns out not to be my first mistake.

When I get the feeling they're about to leave, I pay my tab in cash and ready myself. They're halfway through the door when I stand to follow, and that's when I bump straight into you. I can tell by your expression you're angry, and I need to think and quick. It's too loud in the disco, and so I take you by the hand and lead you outside.

"What the fuck, Jude?" you spit. "You just left me… to come drinking?" You're wild-eyed, and you pant, out of breath, and I watch as my mark turns to see what the commotion is all about. The trail from the disco back to the main part of the hotel and to where the casitas are located is remote, it's dark and desolate, particularly right now. Perfect for killing my mark.

Only there's you—a hormonal, mistaken pregnant woman causing a scene, and now both the mark and his mistress have seen my face. This isn't good. I can't very well whip out my gun and finish the job now. Damn it, Kate, you are a complication I don't need. I tell you as much, and you slap me—and now you have to pay.

WE ARGUE ALL THE WAY BACK TO OUR CASITA. WELL, YOU argue. I walk, dragging you along behind me. Back in our room, I run the shower, lock the door, and get in. I need to think—but more than anything, I need to get away from you. You've lost it. You're like one of those drunken girls, hurling insults at me, accusing me of things I'd never do, and you should ask Amy what happens when a woman can't shut her mouth—and you can't.

As I let the water pour over me, I consider the best way to deal with you. I come up empty-handed.

Eventually, when I retreat from the bathroom, once I've determined nothing more than I'm bad at love and should never have gotten myself into this, I find you sitting on the bed, your phone in your hand.

"I've booked an earlier flight," you tell me and your tone is flat. "I'm leaving. I'm going back home and packing my things. This is over."

"What is wrong with you?" I ask even though I know. You're pregnant and crazy, a bad combination.

"You left me to go drinking. ON OUR HONEYMOON."

"I did not."

You give me the side eye, and then you shake your head. I

go to you and slip the phone out of your hands. You let it go willingly, and I can see you're exhausted. I can see that most of the fight has gone out of you, and you're hoping for a plausible explanation for why you found me in that bar. I decide to give it.

"I was watching a mark."

Your brow furrows. You believe me. Not just because it's the truth but because you're learning to trust just the way I said you would.

I let my towel drop, and I take your hand and stand you up in front of me. I raise your arms and slip your dress over your head. Then I spin you around slowly, gripping your shoulders. I knead them, and you relax into me. "You're too tense," I say, and you sigh.

"Lay down on your stomach," I order, and you do, and you're expecting more. You need more, and so I kneel over you. Then I take your hands in one of mine and stretch them above your head. I grip your sides with my knees as I straddle you. You relax into the bed, into me, and that's when I rear back and deliver the first blow to your ass. Your breath catches and you inhale sharply, then you squirm.

"What the fuck?" you say, and you buck me, but I hold you in place. I bring my palm down again, harder this time. You let out a small scream. Your ass flushes with red.

I lean forward to look directly into your eyes. "You won't ever hit me again. Do you understand?"

"Jude, this isn't funny," and you're trying to get me off, you're trying to move, but there's no give. I'm not hurting you, with the exception of my handprints on your ass. The bed is bearing my weight, and you're furious. I slap the other cheek just as hard and then I take the cuffs from my belt loop. I slowly flip you over onto your back, and I place them around your wrists. You fight the whole time. I'm careful, more careful than I've been with anyone ever. But you need to know you can't one-up me no matter how pregnant you are. I reach around you and unclasp your bra. I remove it, throwing it to the floor, and then I go for masking tape in my bag. You twist, and you turn. You try to break free, but there's no use. You don't scream but you should. Instead, your eyes grow wide, and you say my name, just once, before I place the tape over your mouth.

"You see, Kate. There are certain things about me you need to understand. I'm afraid there are still things I need to teach you. For one, I'm not a cheater. I'm not a drinker. And more than that, I'm not the kind of man one should accuse of such things."

You try to speak against the tape, but all I hear is a garbled mess. I could kill you right now, and a part of me wants to. How else am I going to get rid of you now that the option to turn you in has expired, now that you know so much—now that you're pregnant with my child?

I smile at you. You look pretty lying there. All tied up like a present on Christmas morning. The kind that'll cost you. "You shouldn't underestimate me, sweetheart," I tell you. "I bet your ass is stinging right now, reminding you of this, no?"

You don't respond because you can't, but I can see there's an answer in your eyes, and if I'm not mistaken, a touch of fear.

"You're not the only one who gets to be unpredictable, my dear."

You moan, and you're trying to speak against the tape, and I can't help but laugh a little.

"Breathe through your nose," I advise.

You frown.

"I've always found fighting naked is the best way," I tell you, and your frown remains. I go to you, and I part your legs, and you fight a little, but it doesn't take long before you can't keep it up. When I bring you to this point, I drive it home, by burying my face between your thighs. You may be pissed, but you're wet, and your body gives you away.

Eventually, I make my way up to your eyes, and I can see your anger has faded just a bit. But not completely. Not to worry, though—there's still time to rectify that. I rip off the tape and that hurt. I know it did.

I place my hand over your mouth instead, and you bite down. Hard.

"Do you want me to put the tape back on?" I ask placing my free hand on your throat. I squeeze just hard enough to force you to let go. "Do you want this, Kate? Do you want us?" I demand. I search your eyes, and when I see confirmation in them, I wait. I want your permission for what I have planned. I want to fight without words, to show you how much you need me, and after you nod, I position myself appropriately, and I come into you. Unsurprisingly, you go first.

I WANT YOU TO FEAR ME. YOU NEED TO FEAR ME. OTHERWISE, this won't work. This is why I leave you tied to the bed, and I go out and find my mark. You aren't happy about it, not when I leave and not when I return from completing the kill. It's dangerous being this close to you, as well as staying in the same hotel as the man I just murdered.

That also made it an easy kill. I simply climbed through the window I knew would be left open, and I shot him dead in his sleep all the while his mistress slept soundly next to him. She would say she hadn't heard a thing, and she hadn't, thanks to the silencer, but unfortunately for her, it would take a lot before anyone truly believed her. Not that it mattered much down here. Murdered cartel members are a dime a dozen.

When I get back to the room, you've fallen asleep. "Wake up," I say, jostling you. When your eyes flutter open, I begin throwing our things into our bags hurriedly. I want to be out of here by the time the shit hits the fan. You sit up and watch me.

"We have to go," I say.

"It's a good thing I booked two seats on that early flight," you tell me, and I look up at you, and you're smiling, and I swear with you I never know.

"You get me," I say as I unlock your cuffs.

You stretch your wrists, wring them out, and then you punch me in the gut. Hard. It knocks the wind out of me even though I was almost expecting it.

"So long as you get me too," you say and then you stand on your tippy toes and kiss me, and when I pull back, I taste blood. "You should have let me help."

"I didn't want to ruin our honeymoon with work."

"Well, you did," you tell me, and then you look back toward the bed, and a small smile plays across your lips. "Almost."

You eye your suitcase, and I can see you're searching for your clothes. I point to the chair where I've laid them out for you. "I'm going to go down and check out. You get dressed," I tell you before your face turns pale and you hustle for the bathroom. I grab a room key, listen for a second to you retch, and then I hightail it to the front desk.

When I return, you aren't in the bathroom. In fact, you aren't in our casita at all. I figure you needed water, and so I head for the restaurant, but I don't find you there, either. I check the lobby, you aren't there, and then I head back to our room. Everything is as I left it, only you're nowhere to be found, and so I dial your cell. It goes straight to voicemail.

I'm just about to head back out in search of you when I hear the key card jam in the door.

"Where the hell have you been?" I demand. "We're going to miss our flight."

"I had to see," you say, and my mouth goes dry. Your expression gives nothing away. But you speak calmly, clearly in control. "You didn't kill her," you lament. "Why." It isn't a question.

My legs go numb, there's a ringing in my ears, a humming in my brain. "Kate."

You shrug. "She woke up... what could I do?"

"Kate," I say again, and it's all I can manage.

"She was a cheater, Jude. She deserved it."

You pick up your suitcase. I run my fingers through my hair, and I pace. I can't look at you. I can't meet your eye. I exhale, and I feel you watching. I shake my head. "She was my client's daughter."

~

CHAPTER SIXTEEN

KATE

We've entered unknown territory, and it seems neither of us has a compass much less a map for how to find our way out. We return from our honeymoon, and you are livid with me and rightfully so. When I entered that room in Mexico and smothered that girl, and then hung her body from the rafters, I just wanted you to be proud of me. I wanted you to understand how capable I am—and in a way, I guess you did. Still, it's hard to see you so angry with me. It's hard not to talk with you. We got married, and now nothing feels the same as before. The stakes are higher, but no one knows the rules.

The day after we get back, you pack a bag and take off. You're going to see your client. You need to stay ahead of what's coming, you tell me on your way out the door, and yet so much remains left unsaid.

In the hours after you leave, I go from room to room, organizing and unpacking what little there is to unpack. I sit at the bar, thinking of you, and I should be content, and instead, I'm bored.

I drink my coffee and listen for the washer, and I contemplate my next move. I don't know what that move is, but I do know I've been reduced to listening to the ho-hum of my brand new washing machine, waiting for the load to finish so that I can switch it over, just to give me something to do with my hands. I consider the future, as I study the whooshing sound of the washer and attempt to time my breath to it. I'm not thinking this is the sound I'll hear no fewer than a dozen times a week soon enough, as I wash all those tiny clothes. I should be thinking about the baby, about how to save us. But I'm not.

I'm thinking about how the sound reminds me of the beat, beat, beat of a heartbeat. I imagine that it's my victim's heartbeat, and it's a heartbeat I want to snuff out. The thought of killing consumes me, and it should be enough that I'm here in this house, married to the man of my dreams, pregnant with his child and possibility, but it isn't. And this is when I realize I have a problem.

You've been gone twenty-four hours, and I'm at a loss as to what to do with myself to fill the time. Part of me wonders whether you're ever coming back or whether I've really done it for good this time. I don't want to lose you, but at the same time, I don't want to lose myself either. This isn't who I am, the kind of woman who spends her time roaming from room to room, wondering about a man. I have to fix this or else I have to do something different.

In a last-ditch effort, I went online this afternoon and downloaded all of the best books on how to save a marriage. I don't know if I've found the answer. But I do know one thing, communication is key. That's what all the books say, and we aren't communicating. You shut me out, Jude. You shut me out on our honeymoon, and you're shutting me out now.

But I realized something else from doing this research. I realize I can't make my whole life about you. The books say I need a support system, and I learned that there are certain things only another woman can understand.

I realize it's time to make friends and that pesky redheaded neighbor seems like the easiest place to start.

IT'S DAY THREE, AND YOU'VE ONLY TEXTED TWICE. YOU TOOK the path of least resistance and sent your dad to make sure I'm staying in line, and that was a low blow, so low that I feel like letting you in on the fact that he's not even your real father. But I don't. An eye for an eye makes the whole world blind.

Rudy meets my new friend, and we have plans so he doesn't stay long. Josie is taking me to our neighborhood Bunko night. Who knew there was even such a thing? Well, I, for one, didn't. But I did my research. I now know the game forward and backward and inside out, and I am determined to show these women what I've got. I will not only come home a winner—I will come home with a whole slew of new friends.

I LEARNED THREE VERY IMPORTANT THINGS AT BUNKO NIGHT. One, very little Bunko actually gets played. Two, the women in this neighborhood are competitive, that's for sure, but it has little to do with who wins at Bunko. And three, when you become someone's wife, everyone has an entirely different opinion on what your new role means and how it's supposed to be done.

There are six of us total. I'm told three others are on vacation. I do my best to have a good time, and I even have a small glass of wine, just so these women won't suspect I'm pregnant. It's too soon to know about a honeymoon baby, and Josie has been sworn to secrecy, a secret that's bonded us in a way, and I guess she isn't as bad as I thought. The wine relaxes me, and I don't think about you, mostly because these women like to talk, and I'm good at listening.

Turns out, they have their vices too, and this is what I find most interesting. Ruth, or Ruthie as the girls call her, is having an affair with her high school sweetheart, which she justifies because her husband is away half the time. He's married to his job. Her words. I know a thing or two about that, but my high school sweetheart is dead, and it's probably too soon to tell them about either.

Sharon, she knows a thing about it too. She is married to her work, literally. It's all she talks about. She's an attorney. It's nice to know one, should the need arise, but she name drops like nothing I've ever seen, and the wine makes her brave. I know all of her life's accomplishments in three minutes flat.

Anne's vice is her charity work. She sits on half a dozen boards and swears she's changing the world. But from what I can see, she mostly excels at talking down to people.

Then there's sweet Angie. Angie collects children like some people collect stamps. She's currently pregnant with her fourth, and she's made it her sole mission in life to reproduce, no less than the best, like she's going for some sort of award. The entirety of her existence these days revolves around preschool applications and excelling at pregnancy, and I secretly wonder how many ways you can get it wrong. She's fascinating in her strive for perfection. You would like that about her. But there's the other side you would probably hate: Angie creates meditation tapes for her mommy group. They're supposed to help with achieving the perfect whatever, and I realize I have so much to learn. I wonder if you'd hang around if I became a little more like her.

Josie has a husband and a baby, I learn, although I've hardly heard her mention her spouse—and not once has she talked about the baby. Josie is excellent at listening, at being an ear and a friend, and I can't help but notice there's more to her than I originally thought.

YOU'RE GONE FOUR DAYS, AND YOU COME HOME WITHOUT warning. When I return home from a charity luncheon that Anne invited me to, I'm surprised to find you in your office.

You don't ask where I've been. You simply stand, walk around the desk, plant your mouth on mine and usher me backward, laying me flat across your desk. Then you push my dress up over my hips, and you show me what forgiveness feels like.

THE FOLLOWING MORNING, YOU TELL ME OVER COFFEE THAT your client seems to have bought that someone got to the mark and the client's daughter first. Obviously, you've vowed to find this person. You don't tell me you went with the intention of killing your client, but I know you better than you think.

I tell you about my new friends and you half-listen, you're distracted, and you aren't making your usual effort to hide it. I don't tell you I'm distracted too. I don't tell you that the urge to kill is stronger than ever or that I'm going to have to do something about it—sooner rather than later. I don't tell you that I don't know what to do with my hands, that I've forgotten how to just be. I don't tell you about the anxiety of trying to fit in here or how it's so different than I expected. I tell you other things, though, things I've read in the pregnancy books, but you know it all, you've been reading too.

"Promise me you won't kill again," you say, and it catches me off guard.

I look at you, and I don't know where this is coming from, and looking back, I can't say I saw it coming. I thought you loved me because we are the same, and now all you want is for me to be different. "I—I..." I try to speak, I try to answer, but words elude me.

You cock your head, and you study me. Suddenly, I see how exhausted you look. How troubled. "Kate—come on. At least not until after the baby comes..."

I swallow.

"Can you just promise me that? Is it really so much to ask?"

I want to tell you yes, that it is a lot to ask. That I'm already giving up so much of what makes me, me being here in this house, trying to make friends with women I hardly like. I want to tell you it feels like my body, and now my mind is being invaded—that I'm losing control of everything, all at once. But more than that, I want to tell you that I can stop. I want it to be true.

But it isn't. I wish I could forget the feeling of a kill. The euphoria. The thrill. But I can't. It's a part of me. Sometimes it seems that it's all of me and that the further away I get from my last kill, the more of me the murderer within consumes. And while there are a million things to think about—like my new friends or bunko night or the charity event I've agreed to host—this sick need eats away at me until there's nothing left. It's gnawing from the inside, begging to be let out. I want to tell you this, but I don't know how. Not when you've been so angry with me. Not when I know how bad I've messed up. Not when I know that the choice is you or it.

"Kate," you say, and your voice is stern. "I *need* you to promise me."

"Okay," I relent, and I make my choice. "I promise."

You nod and then you come to me. You wrap your arms around my waist and then you kiss the top of my head. "I love you," you say and then you take your coffee and leave, taking a piece of me when you go.

MONTHS PASS. MY BELLY GROWS ROUNDER, AND I REACH THE mid-point in my second trimester. I don't kill anyone, but that doesn't mean I'm not making a list. You're gone a lot for work. You tell me it's so that you can slow down when the baby comes. But I'm not so sure. I help you a little bit in your searches here and there, but I can't help but feel a bit removed. My marriage books say it's important to keep some distance in a marriage. They say it isn't wise to mix love and business, and since I've promised not to kill, there's a bigger part of me that can't stomach knowing you still get to do it. You still get to have your fun. Nothing changes for you. Everything changed for me. I know I'm supposed to be grateful—after all, this is what every girl dreams of, isn't it? But I'm not. And I don't recall sitting in this empty house all alone being a part of any dream I've ever had.

This is why I've thrown myself into planning a Christmas charity ball where wealthy people pay twelve hundred dollars a plate to help underprivileged youth. I excel at getting sponsors for the event—a task which turns out to be a full-time job. But the more I get into planning, the more questions I have about the way this whole thing works. Something about the math isn't adding up. Anne blows me off each time I go to her with these questions, and eventually, she stops returning my calls altogether.

So I do what I have to do to make the numbers right, even if that means limiting the open bar to two drinks per plate—it's not like it'll affect me anyway, but this is about the kids. I also cancel the band and change the menu to hors d'oeuvres only.

The day of the event, you call to say your flight has been delayed, and it looks like you won't make it home in time. In fact, it looks like you won't make it home until morning, and while this is disappointing, I can't say it's surprising. I don't tell you this, though. There's too much to do here. I have a handyman coming to paint the nursery and still a ton of last-minute preparations to make for tonight.

THE PHONE RINGS, AND I'M EXPECTING A CALL FROM THE caterer, but it's you.

"I just want to apologize again," you say, and you sound tired. "I hate it that I can't be there."

"It's fine," I assure you. Meanwhile, I'm knee deep in color swatches.

"It isn't fine, Kate," you argue. "And you know how much I hate that word."

I sigh. My dress is fitting tighter than it's meant to, and I can't breathe. The handyman is taking longer than he promised and now there's you. The baby flips and I tell you about it. The kicks are just now getting strong enough for you to feel but, you haven't caught one yet. It's a game we play, trying to time it, and I swear our baby already knows the art of evasion.

"I miss you, Kate."

"I miss you too," I say. "But you'll be home in the morning. And then you can feel it for yourself."

"I want to bring you back into the business," you throw out, and it surprises me. "Like we planned."

The handyman comes in and mouths the word hammer. I don't tell you about the handyman. I know you'll be mad. You wanted to paint the baby's room, but it hasn't gotten done, and I wanted to prove a point. I hold up my index finger asking for a minute.

"I'd like to hear more about that," I tell you. "But listen… I've gotta run."

"I love you."

"Love you too," I reply, and then I smile even though I know you can't see. "I'll see you in the morning," I tell you, and I hang up first. Afterward, I go into the garage to grab a hammer from your toolbox. I've asked the handyman to hang a painting I ordered. It's a surprise, and I'm doing my best to stay productive in ways you'll notice. Buying expensive artwork seems to get your attention. Anyway, as I'm digging around, I find a small photo album in the bottom of your toolbox. What I find knocks the wind out of me. You didn't tell me Amy was beautiful, Jude. But I guess I should have known. Also, these pictures, they weren't taken in Sri Lanka.

~

"WHAT. IN. THE. HELL. IS. GOING. ON, KATE?" ANNE seethes. She throws up her hands for effect, and she's wearing a backless dress that screams 'I've got money.' Everyone stares. She's the kind of woman that's hard not to look at, even when she isn't causing a scene. "This is not what we planned!"

I shrug. "I wanted the money to go to the kids," I tell her. "Like we promised. That meant cutting a few things…"

She shakes her head slowly from side to side for maximum effect. "There are card tables, for heaven's sake, and plastic chairs. THIS ISN'T A BACKYARD BAR-B-QUE!"

She grabs my arm and tries to usher me aside. I dig my heels in. Literally. I do not budge. "I ran the numbers," I tell her. "They don't add up."

"The numbers are none of your business," she spits. She looks from side to side to see who's listening. Everyone, of course.

"I've worked for months, thinking I was helping children when all I was really doing was planning a fancy party for your friends."

"That is the point of charity, Kate. That's how you raise money."

"But what about the kids," I ask, and my hand goes instinctively to my stomach. "What do they get out of it?"

We have a crowd, Anne and I, and it's growing by the minute. We're head-to-head, squared off toe-to-toe, and she looks like a pit-viper ready to strike a pregnant woman, so I gather that makes the whole thing a little more interesting. I've embarrassed her. I've called her out. I know what I've done, and maybe there are more ways than I realized to kill a person.

"You need to leave, Kate." she seethes. "Now."

I stand up a little straighter, and she takes aim. "I don't know if this white trash way of doing things is just your nature, but I'll never—"

"Let's go," Josie tells me taking me by the hand. "No need to be mean. This isn't the end of the world," she says looking at Anne.

"The hell it isn't. You brought this trash into our circle, and I told you, I TOLD YOU she wouldn't fit in with us. I told you she couldn't hack it. I mean, *come on*, Josie. What kind of person invites strangers to their wedding? I'll tell you —new money—the kind that doesn't have friends above trailer park level, that's who. She didn't even know us. And it was her wedding, for Christ's sake. Some things are sacred. But not new money. Obviously. She tried too hard. From the very beginning. Don't you remember? I tried to warn you," Anne says, looking around at the group of Bunko ladies. "But you wouldn't listen… none of you listened! Now, look what you've done. Look at this mess. She's trying to bring us down to her level. "

"That's enough, Anne," Josie says before she turns and leads me to the door.

"I hope you don't think this is the end of this, Kate," Anne calls back over her shoulder. "You don't get to embarrass me and get away with it."

I can't help but smile. She is right about at least one thing she said. This is far from over.

WHEN I GET HOME, I CRAWL STRAIGHT INTO BED. I'M exhausted. I don't fall asleep plotting Anne's murder as I surely would have once upon a time. I drift off thinking of you, thinking of seeing your face, of telling you all about tonight, and of getting to the bottom of that terrible mess I discovered in the garage.

IT'S THE SHARP TASTE OF METALLIC THAT I NOTICE FIRST. There's no denying the taste. It can always only be one thing. Blood.

I feel pain, and then there's a blow. To my head, I think.

But I can't be sure. I can't get a grip on it. My ears ring and everything is dark. I feel my throat constrict as my mouth fills with blood, I'm trying to say something or maybe I'm trying to scream. I can't be sure. My heart races, and I think I feel the baby move. She moves most at night. I wish you were here to feel it. I wish I would wake up to find you here holding me when this nightmare ends, but then I remember you aren't.

I don't know if it's still dark outside or whether my eyes fail me, but I don't like this dream, and when I feel myself slipping back into the comfort of sleep, I willingly go with it.

THERE ARE BRIGHT LIGHTS, AND I AM SCREAMING, BEGGING, pleading. This isn't happening. I can't see much, just a sliver of a flurry of people, working above me. My eyes are heavy and matted shut. But I do know the room is cold, and it smells familiar—of antiseptic and bleach. I also know what happens next because they've just told me. I shut my eyes so I don't have to watch. I will myself to slip backward into the darkness, anything to stop what is happening. But I don't slip. The room is spinning, and the lights are too bright, even with my eyes shut, and they're holding me down, rattling off medical jargon I can't understand.

I ask for you, and they tell me not to worry, they will help me.

But I know better.

Nothing can help me now.

They are liars.

I'M LYING ON A GURNEY STARING AT THE CEILING. I'M BEING whisked down a long corridor. I say your name aloud, just to see if I can, but there's no sound, and someone pats my head, but it isn't you.

I want to ask about the baby, but I can't keep my eyes open.

I'm fading, and I feel a pain I can't name. It aches all the way down to my bones, and somehow, somewhere deep down, I know this, even though I can't pinpoint its exact location. It's searing, tearing me in two, and I wonder if you know.

I wonder why aren't you here.

You should be here.

∾

CHAPTER SEVENTEEN

JUDE

We came together in the summer, married in the fall, but winter inevitably came, as winter always does. Winter left us cold, withered, dead. It's raining and wet out, fitting, and altogether nasty, but I am en route to the hospital within three minutes of getting Josie's call. She's found you barely alive and barely breathing, but she doesn't tell me this, not exactly. It doesn't matter. All I can think about is you and the baby and making whatever happened ok.

Later, at the hospital, I get the full story. It takes me too long to get there, and I am a mess. Josie tells the police who tell me that she was worried about you after what happened at your charity function and wanted to make sure you were all right. When you didn't answer the door or her calls, she used the key I'd given her to let herself in. Thank God she did. She caught the bastard who did what he did to you, rummaging through our house, our things, but not before he could get away.

The old lady who lives down the street, the one who's always watching, the one you swear gives you the stink-eye, she saw the guy fleeing on foot. He was parked in front of her drive, and so she memorized his plates. She has a thing about people parking in front of her house. Thank God, she does. Thanks to her, the cops stopped him a mere three miles away.

WHEN THEY FINALLY LET ME SEE YOU, YOU DON'T WAKE UP, not for a long time. I start to worry that you might not, but they assure me this is normal given your injuries. I have a lot of time to think here in this room. It's small, and it's closing in on me. There are machines keeping you alive, and I think of all the times I've wanted to kill you myself, and now here you are so close to death that I'm physically sick. What's worse is there's nothing to do but listen to the hum of the machines and wait. But while I wait, I plot. I want to know how this happened and why—but more than anything, I want to take care of the man who did it. Justice is always best served by those who deserve it most. And I intend to serve it well.

The detectives who've been assigned to the case tell me the man isn't speaking. They suspect robbery was his motive. But I know better. We can't be that unlucky. Although luck— or whether he talks or he doesn't—matters little. The only thing that matters now is justice, and I promise you I intend to pursue it swiftly and relentlessly.

YOUR EYELIDS FLUTTER SLOWLY AND THEN, AT ONCE, THEY open. You wince, and your arm instinctively moves toward your stomach, but they have you tethered due to the trach tube. You frown the moment you understand you can't move, and there's nowhere to go anyway. The bastard busted your windpipe, and you can't speak, but your eyes tell me what you want to know.

"I'm sorry. The baby didn't make it," I tell you as matter of factly as possible, as though the words aren't ripping me in two. I've prepared for this for hours, repeating it over and over to take the sting out, and I hope it worked.

Your eyes well up with tears, and then you close them and drift off. I hope you dream, and I hope that wherever you are when you slip back into sleep that it is far away from the reality that awaits you here in the ICU.

THE NEXT TIME YOU OPEN YOUR EYES, IT'S WITH A START. YOU panic. There's a level of fear in your expression I've never seen before. You're here in this room, but you're somewhere else too—somewhere dark and far away. My voice does little to comfort you. In fact, it doesn't touch you at all. Alarms chime, the nurse comes in, and finally, she injects something into your IV.

"She's not ready yet," she tells me. I study the monitor. I know how the numbers should read, and I will them to go there. Meanwhile, the nurse talks to me about stuff, normal everyday stuff as though there is life outside of these hospital walls. I half listen just in case she says something that pertains to you.

I don't say anything because what is there to say?

THE NEXT FEW DAYS ARE MOSTLY THE SAME. THE DOCTORS DO this bad news/good news thing that drives me insane. The latest is that there might be brain damage, but it's too soon to tell. The good news, they say, is there aren't any brain bleeds.

Your pelvis is shattered, but you should be able to walk again in time.

Your windpipe will heal, but your voice may never sound the same.

The temporary pins in your left leg will come out, and they'll replace them with something better, something permanent. The other broken bones will heal on their own. The body is good at healing.

But what about the rest of you? Will that heal? I ask a lot of questions, but not these because I know no one has the answers. Maybe not even you.

～

THEY WEAN YOU OFF THE VENT, AND YOU FIGHT IT ALL THE way. You don't like the restraints, but it's hospital policy. They tell me it's for your protection. You tear the skin off your wrists when you struggle against the cuffs. I plead with you to settle down, but you can't hear me. The nurses say it's the medication—that you don't understand there's another choice, and seeing you like this, it's almost too much to take.

～

YOU WAKE UP SLOWLY. YOUR EYES TRAIL TOWARD YOUR stomach. I've had lots of practice this time. "The baby didn't make it. I'm sorry," I tell you.

You look away. You're far off again. Here. But not.

I don't tell you the baby was a girl. That she never had a chance. I don't tell you that she died in utero as a result of blows inflicted by a madman. Your hands and arms have extensive defensive wounds. You fought like hell. I do tell you that.

YOU WAKE UP AND ASK THE SAME QUESTION WITH YOUR EYES, and I swear it's like fucking Groundhog's Day. I tell you the baby didn't make it, and you slip off to someplace I can't go. Part of me wants to lie, to see if you'll stay. But I don't have it in me. The truth is the best I've got.

That's not to say I tell you everything. I don't.

I can't.

Not yet.

YOU SPEND THREE WEEKS IN THE HOSPITAL. AND OVER THREE weeks, the truth trickles in a little bit more. Your milk comes in, but there's no baby to feed. You bleed, but there's no reward for it in the end. One day, when I'm almost ready to deliver the news, you catch me by surprise. The truth has a way of seeping in unexpectedly that way.

"I'm not going to be able to have children, am I?" You ask looking directly at me, something you've rarely done over the past eighteen days, and it's not a question, not really.

"The doctors say probably not."

"When were you going to tell me?"

"I don't know," I tell you, and it's the truth.

YOU DON'T WANT TO COME HOME AND IT'S BEST THAT WAY. WE get you moved to a rehabilitation hospital, and they won't let me stay there overnight, but I stay as long as I can. Most nights, they have to force me to leave. You don't talk much, but I bring you books that you pretend to read. We go on like this for so long it almost starts to feel normal.

S<small>URPRISINGLY</small>, <small>YOU DON'T ASK ABOUT THE MONSTER WHO DID</small> this. You don't seek answers as to why this has happened, and I think that's what scares me the most. He's being taken care of, I told you once, shortly after you first woke up, and that seemed to be enough for you, even though it isn't. How could it be?

N<small>OT THAT YOU ASK</small>, <small>BUT THE GUY'S NAME IS</small> S<small>HAWN</small> G<small>ORDON</small>, and he has a rap sheet a mile long, which isn't a surprise. The cops tell me he mentioned ties to an old girlfriend of mine, but they don't think the connection warrants anything more than making us easy targets. He isn't talking either, not much, anyway. The police still believe his motive was burglary with the intent of sexual assault, although you kept him busy enough that he didn't quite get around to the second part. But he did rape us in other ways, didn't he, Kate?

He raped and pillaged and stole more than just items from our home. He took things that can never be replaced, things that can never be given back.

This is why I have Bob send a guy in after him even though I wanted to do it myself. Bob says I'm too close to the case to handle it, and for the first time, I almost agree. But I don't want to make death easy for Gordon. I don't want it to look pretty. I need it to be quick before I do something stupid. But not too quick. Bob assures me it won't be.

You spend thirteen weeks in rehab healing and learning to walk again and trying to regain most of the functionality you've lost. You're a good patient—or so they say. You don't ask for much, and you don't talk to the shrink when he makes his rounds. You're determined, this much I can see. I visit a lot even when you ask me not to come every day. I come anyway. Sometimes you even talk to me. Mostly, you don't.

Until one day you do. I'm putting away your laundry; you're staring out the window. It's our new normal. Until it isn't.

"I saw those photos you keep in the garage. Of Amy."

"What photos?" I ask even though I know exactly what photos.

You sigh slowly. "The ones that weren't taken in Sri Lanka. The ones that were taken here. In Austin."

"She visited once," I say, stuffing your pants in a drawer.

"They were more recent than you let on."

I shrug.

"Jude," you say, and your voice is sharp. "Why did you lie to me?"

I don't meet your eye. I could tell you, but this time, it's me who's not ready.

"Jude," you say again, only your voice is lower this time.

"Where is she?"

"I don't know," I tell you.

But we both know it isn't the truth.

I HAVEN'T WORKED MUCH AT ALL OVER THE PAST FOUR months. I let Rudy handle my cases, but I can tell he is growing just as weary and antsy as I am. It is time, he assures me the last time I call for help. He is right, it is time, and so I accepted the case. It takes me out of town for three days, three days that will give me enough time to decide what to do about the Amy situation. Three days that will give you a break from my hovering. Maybe a break is what we need, I decide. And so I go.

IT SHOULDN'T HAVE SURPRISED ME THAT WHEN I RETURN, YOU are gone, but it does. You left a note tucked into a book at the front desk. *Gone Girl.* How fitting. The note says you need answers, but even more than that, you need space.

Space can mean a lot of things to a lot of people, I guess. Sort of like how I thought three days was a break, and you took it to mean you could make your break. Space is subjective, it turns out.

Two months later, I receive divorce papers. And I have to admit I don't know exactly what I was expecting. But, I can tell you—it wasn't quite that much space.

CHAPTER EIGHTEEN

KATE

South America has always had a way of welcoming me with open arms, and so it seems as good a place as any to lay low, to get my bearings back. I suspect that you might try and find me, but when weeks pass, and you don't, I take it that you aren't going to. You're hiding something, and as a general rule, people who are hiding things don't go around trying to be found.

A month passes, and you could have called, you could've emailed, but you don't, and so when the second month comes and goes, and it's only more of the same, I figure what's done is done.

I gave you an out, and you took it. I can't hate you for that even though I do, just a little. You, at least, can still have children, and you should. You shouldn't give that up for me, and I wouldn't let you if you tried. That's why I'm here, and you're there. That's why you aren't trying. I don't blame you. I just want off this ride. I want to break the cycle. I want a new start, and I want to give you yours.

Looking back, it's quite easy to see the error of your ways

once the mistake has been made. I made many. I gave up so much for you—and not just my ability to bear children. I changed who I was, fundamentally, in order to make you happy, and in doing so, I let my guard down. Look where it led me.

Right back here where I started.

Only worse.

~

ONCE THE DIVORCE IS FILED, I DECIDE IT'S TIME TO GET BACK on the horse, so to speak, and I start dating again. More like dabbling, than anything.

I also start a little side project. For our daughter. For all the things she won't get to see—for all of the things she won't get to be.

I know there is more to the story than that man just breaking into our home to steal a few things. I know because he nearly beat me to death, killing our baby in the process, which ceased all hope for any kind of future we might've had.

I've pored over and over the police reports, the jail incident report of his death for clues, the chance to find anything I don't already know. Maybe I'll never know exactly *why* he did what he did, but I do know at least three things: One, he started with violence against women early on in his career. Two, I wasn't his first trip to the rodeo. And three, he had ties to Amy.

The fact that he started early and that he was a registered sex offender is what set things in motion, things that help me heal. *Almost.*

South America, like most countries these days, has a huge issue with child trafficking. I may not have been able to save our daughter, Jude. But I can save someone else's.

The dating isn't going well.
No one is you.
For better or worse.

BUT THE MURDERING—NOW THAT IS GOING EXQUISITELY. I'VE seen enough Dateline NBC to know how this works. These men are perverts—but they are nearly all the same. Same excuses. Same MO.

Because I'm still healing, I've taken to your method of killing. A single shot. Turns out, that's all it takes. But I have to say, it's not quite as fun—although it'll do for now.

YOU RECEIVED THE DIVORCE PAPERS TODAY AND THEN YOU called. I was at the beach watching the maid's kids play and couldn't bring myself to answer. But then, really, what more is there to say?

Well, according to the email you sent, quite a lot.

To: Kate Anderson

From: Jude

Subject: Vows

You can't have a divorce. You said 'till death do us part.

That means one of us has to die.

Love,

Jude

Being politically correct has never been your strong suit. You seem to miss the fact that I did, in fact, almost die. I can't help myself. I write back.

To: Jude
From: Kate Anderson
Subject: Re: Vows

Wrong. I made sure those words were specifically not in our wedding vows.

Kate

To: Kate Anderson
From: Jude
Subject: Re: Re:Vows

I don't care. One of us is going to have to die before I grant you a divorce.

I miss you.

Love,
Jude

To: Jude
From: Kate Anderson
Subject: Re: Re: Re: Vows

Over your dead body, then.

Kate

YOU DON'T WRITE BACK AFTER THAT. NEITHER DO I. THE NEXT time I see you is in court, and we both know how that turns out.

CHAPTER NINETEEN

JUDE

We're due back at the therapist's office in four days, and I'll admit I've stalked you a little, I have. You're back in that funky apartment, well, the same complex anyway, different unit. I watch you, and I can't help but get the sense you're annoyed that you're stuck here for the duration of the judge's terms, but you carry on with business like it's nothing. You impress me, just as you always have, and it's always been the side of you I see when you think I'm not looking that I like best.

I follow you to the outskirts of town to a plot of land, which holds nothing but an old barn. I can't figure it out at first. It's dilapidated, falling down. But you go there often, sometimes in the dark and sometimes in the light of day, and you've always excelled at keeping me on my toes. It doesn't take me long to see that you lure men there. All sex offenders. I know because I run their plates. You play hide and seek, but they never find you, not until later when you're in their home, and even then, you're not what they were expecting. Why not just kill them there? These are things I'd ask you if now was before, but I've learned a few lessons too. I'd be gentler about it. But not that gentle because, even though you've evolved in your method of killing, you aren't being particularly careful about it. A part of me thinks you want to be caught, and this is how I know it has to be me doing the catching.

~

TWO DAYS BEFORE OUR SECOND THERAPY APPOINTMENT, I FIND the answers to all of our problems. Well, at least half of them, anyway. Spring has finally arrived, although I can't say it feels much like it. I am on my way to a dinner downtown, which is actually a job interview of sorts, but that is a story for another day, and anyway, I never made it to the interview. Maybe someday I will.

There's a chill in the air as I walk down the street. The wind is biting and cold, and it looks every bit as much like March as it feels. I'm not certain about the dinner meeting. I've always worked for myself or for Rudy in the early days, and going with a firm seems like a cop-out now. So when it starts to rain, I take it as a sign. I need to turn around. I haven't brought an umbrella, and there's no point in showing up soaking wet to a business dinner where competence is key. But I don't turn around, not right away; I keep walking and thinking of you, and this is when I see the answer.

Twenty feet in front of me, huddled together on the sidewalk, sits a young woman and a baby. I watch as people pound the payment. They walk on, around them, stepping off the curb and onto the street to avoid doing anything, and it's as though they're invisible. But they aren't, not to me. When I reach where they are huddled, I squat down. The baby squawks.

"Do you need help?" I ask the girl.

She doesn't meet my eye. So I take my time, studying her

face, and I determine she can't be more than seventeen if that.

"It's cold out," I say, and this time, she meets my gaze. I can see in her eyes she wants to say 'no shit it's cold.' She's living in it, so she knows, but she doesn't say it—she isn't sure. Instead, she jostles the baby in her arms, and its cries grow louder.

"Your baby seems cold," I tell her trying a different approach. I study the baby closely with its wind-burned cheeks. Its brown eyes are as wide as saucers. I don't know a lot about infants, but if I had to guess, I'd say he looks to be about four months old or so, and I want to tell her the streets are no place for a baby, but I know this girl realizes that. I just don't think she knows what to do about it.

"He's cute," I add when she doesn't answer.

"It's a SHE," the girl tells me, exasperated. If she knew how little I know about babies, I don't think she'd be so offended. Nonetheless, this girl isn't one to go easy on either, and so I glance at the blue onesie the baby is wearing. She follows my gaze and pulls the baby in closer. She reads my mind. She likes hardball. "Yeah, well. Beggars can't be choosy, can they? That's what my mother always said."

"No, I guess they can't," I tell her, and I reach for my wallet. Then I think better of it. "Listen," I say. "There's a motel about three blocks from here."

"I'm not into that, mister,"

"What?"

"I don't do that."

"Oh," I say, and I purse my lips. "Well, I don't either," I assure her. "I'm married," I tell her, flashing the wedding band I can't bring myself to take off.

She gives me a look. "When has that ever mattered?"

"It matters to me," I say, and I watch as she sticks her filthy pinky into the baby's mouth, and it begins sucking furiously. She stops crying but only for a second, and she starts up again. Her wails are piercing, and I'd do just about anything to make it stop. "I tell you what…I will pay for a room for you, for tonight if you have nowhere else to go."

"Does it look like I have any other place to go?"

I don't answer. I should watch how I phrase things, but the crying, it's throwing me off. "What will you do tomorrow?" I ask.

"God always provides," she tells me, her face blank.

"But what about the baby? Do you have food? Diapers…I don't know…do you have all the things babies need?"

She gives me that look again.

I exhale. "I'll leave some money at the front desk of the motel on South Congress. You know the one?

I wait for a response, but she only nods. I can tell she isn't sure so I jot down the address, and then I stand to go.

When I turn my back, she clears her throat. "God bless you, mister," she calls out into the biting wind. I don't turn back in spite of myself.

FIRST, I VISIT THE ATM AND THEN THE MOTEL. AFTER THAT, I go home, having determined I'm unable and unwilling to concede to working for someone else. I like making my own rules, and it's a little late to change that now. When I finally climb into bed, for the first night in as long as I can remember, I don't fall asleep thinking about you. In fact, I find that I can't fall asleep at all.

I can't stop thinking about the girl and her baby. Eventually, when I realize sleep isn't going to come, I get up and go to our baby's half-finished room. There are a few outfits hanging in the closet. I remembered them in the dark. Now, I run my fingers along the fabric, and I remember the look on your face when you showed them to me. I don't know if they'll fit the girl's baby, but I figure I can't sleep anyway, and it's worth a shot.

I make the trek back downtown. The guy manning the front desk has a man bun, and he gives zero fucks about telling me exactly what room the girl and the baby are in. "Damn thing won't quit crying," he tells me. "We've already had to move two guests, and we're outta rooms."

"Babies cry," I say. He looks up at me, and he shrugs and points toward the door. "It's that way."

I knock on the girl's door, and I hear her call from inside. "It's about damn time," she huffs as she throws the door open. Her face falls when she sees I'm not who she was expecting.

"It's you," she says.

"It's me," I tell her, pushing the door open fully. I survey the room, starting with her bloodshot eyes, moving on to the empty liquor bottle, and then the one sitting next to it that looks as though it's just been opened. "God provides," I say as I make my way in. I kick the door closed behind me with my heel.

"Pablo will be here any minute," she assures me, and I can see the fear in her eyes.

"I bet he will."

"Where's the baby?" I ask, searching the room, and she hesitates for a second but then she points to the bathroom. I follow her gaze. "She likes sleeping in the tub. You know what they say about babies and small spaces..."

I look back at her, and my face grows hot. She can tell I'm not happy as I eye the needle hanging out of her vein. She touches the syringe as though she's forgotten it's there, as though I haven't just interrupted her little party. "How long have you been using?"

She shrugs.

"Is the baby addicted? Is that why it cries all the time?"

She narrows her brow. "Do you know *anything* about babies?"

"Not really," I admit.

The girl eyes me up and down, and then she waves me off. "She's fine."

"I hate that word. And she doesn't sound fine," I say, trying to peek into the bathroom just to make sure. It's all I can do not to bust in and scoop her up. I take a step toward the door. I don't want to scare her, but I need to see for myself. The girl reads my expression, and then she throws up her hands. The syringe springs from side to side, but it doesn't fall out. It's actually quite impressive the way it just hangs there. She sees me looking, and she shakes her head. She shoves past me and goes to the tub. "Oh," she says as she leans down and picks up the baby. "You're awake." I strain to get a look.

"What do you want?" the girl asks me when she gets back out into the small entryway. It's too small a space for the three of us, and she reeks. Both of them do, actually. I move away as she juggles the baby who is clearly wide-awake and has been for some time. It's then she seems to recall she has a needle dangling from her arm.

"Can I hold the baby?"

She shrugs and then she gladly hands her over.

She flops down on the far double bed and then reaches over and deftly injects her poison. I watch as she removes the needle and lets it fall to the floor. She looks directly at me. "Why are you here?"

"What's her name?"

"She doesn't have one."

"What do you mean, she doesn't have one?"

She shrugs again. "I wanted to get to know her first…"

"How long does that take?" I ask and the baby peers at me.

She doesn't cry, but I can tell she wants to. She's probably all cried out.

"Has she eaten?"

"Of course, she's eaten," the girl spits, her tone a mixture of inebriated and annoyed. She gestures toward an empty bottle on the bedside table. "What kind of mother do you think I am?"

I don't answer.

"How much for the baby?" I ask instead.

She gasps. But I don't think she's altogether shocked. I guess being high will do that to you. "I'm not selling you my child."

"A grand? Two grand?"

She cocks her head to the side. "Wait, you mean like two-thousand dollars?"

"That's exactly what I mean."

She looks away then, out the sliding glass door, and this is how I know I'm close. This is her tell. She looks away when it really matters. Like most people.

"It would get you off the streets," I tell her.

She looks back at me then and then at the baby. "Are you serious?"

"As a heart attack."

The girl eyes me up and down, I stare at the baby, and for the first time, I notice how light she feels in my arms. Meanwhile, I can tell her mother is wondering if I'm the kind of person who has that kind of money when it seems so far out of her reach. I can also tell that she believes I am, and I can see she doubts such a small sum could mean so little to me when it has the potential to change her whole world. She doesn't realize that I would offer more if she demanded it because it has the potential to change my whole world too.

Of course, she's likely to use the money on drugs, but that's beside the point.

"There's one condition," I say.

She folds her lips and stares at the floor, and for the second time, I realize how very young she looks.

"You have to meet me at my attorney's office to sign the paperwork. When you do, I'll have your cash for you."

"That's it?"

"Is there something else?"

"Ummm…" she utters, and she shifts on the bed. Yes," she eventually says, and she looks around the room. Her eyes are shifty, and I can tell she's not sure, but also, that she's probably too high to care. "Can you take her tonight?" She bites her lip, and I can see that it's starting to bleed. "Pablo's on his way… and well, he doesn't like babies."

"Is Pablo the father?"

"Of course not. Her father's dead."

"Oh," I say. "Can you prove that?" I ask. I lay the baby on the bed. I don't think she's old enough to move, but I don't go far, just in case as I gather her things, just a blanket, a bottle, and a package of diapers. The girl hands me a plastic bag labeled hotel laundry, and I stuff the items in it.

"Wait. She has formula," she offers as she opens the small refrigerator. I nod, and I glance over at the baby. She hasn't moved.

"She can't roll over yet," the girl says, and I swear she's a natural at reading people, even high, and it makes me sad to know that she's learned the hard way. "She's only three months."

I nod, and then I jot my cell phone number down on the motel stationary. "Her father," I say again. "Can you prove he's dead?"

She crosses her arms and then shakes her head as though I'm the dumbest person on the planet. "Sure as hell can. It was in every paper. He was one of those pedophiles they found shot cold."

I swallow hard, and I realize that some things are meant to be.

OUR FIRST NIGHT TOGETHER IS A DISASTER. FOUR HOURS IN, and I'm flat out exhausted. When I can no longer keep my eyes open, and I realize I know less about babies than I imagined, which wasn't much to begin with, I ring Josie.

She comes right over, and best of all, she knows exactly what to do.

First, I sleep, and then we come up with a plan.

They say babies can't save a marriage. But they are wrong.

CHAPTER TWENTY

KATE

There's a knock at my door, only I'm not expecting anyone, least of all Josie. We haven't really spoken, not since the last time she visited me in rehab. But that was before I left and before I quit talking to anyone, including you. I see her standing there, full of hope, and so I do the only thing that makes sense. I open the door wider and invite her in, even though I don't want to. I figure it's the least I can do, given that she saved my life.

"How's the little one?" I ask. Not because I genuinely want to know, but because I can't think of anything else to say.

"He's great," she says, and her face beams, and it's just one more reminder in a sea of many that I'll never know that look.

I watch as she plops down on my cheap futon, and I can't help but feel slightly embarrassed that this place is such a far cry from what she's used to. But mostly I feel nothing.

I stand back, unsure of what to do with myself with someone else in my space. But unlike me, Josie seems sure of herself—she always has come to think of it—and I watch as she crosses her legs and folds her hands in her lap. I brace myself as she gives me a look that I'm certain will haunt me for some time, and I think I know exactly what comes next.

"Jude misses you, you know. He talks about you all the time."

That was exactly what I thought she'd say. It sucker punches me, nonetheless. I want to tell her that it's not that I don't miss you too, it's not as though I've just flipped a switch and turned off the love I felt, but it's something more. I want to tell her that I can't trust you because I suspect you've done something to your ex-girlfriend, only this doesn't seem to fall within the confines of everyday neighborly conversation. So I can't really tell her that, can I?

I can't tell her that a part of me wonders if you're capable of doing the same to me. So I simply swallow the words, the feelings. I swallow the piece of me that sides somewhere with the truth.

"Yes, well—" I start but then I can't think of anything that will complete the sentence. I can't let her in, not really. If I can't trust you, who can I trust? Certainly not the neighbor girl.

I don't meet her glare, but it's burning a hole through me. I hear her inhale, and I listen as she lets it out. "The thing is, Kate... Love doesn't come around like this every day. You guys were happy. You know you were. I saw it. Hell, everybody saw it...we were there at your wedding and—"

"Things change," I say, cutting her off.

"What things?"

"Our baby is dead, for one," I tell her, and it's the first time I've ever said it aloud, and it's a blow to the gut. I can't breathe.

"I saw Jude," she says. She doesn't wait for me to recover. She's hell-bent on driving the nail in the coffin. "Yesterday in the grocery store. I nearly ran into him with my cart."

I can't tell if she's telling the truth. But I don't say anything. I just want her to go.

"He has a baby, Kate."

I look up at her then. "What?" I ask, and my voice catches in my throat.

"Jude adopted a baby. He says he hopes you'll come home."

"He what?" I ask again. I lean backward against the wall, looking for something, anything to steady me. I massage my temples. The room is spinning, and I'm pretty sure I can't see straight.

Josie walks over to where I'm hunched against the wall, and she places her hand on my arm so lightly that she might as well not have been touching me at all. "There's a baby girl waiting for you at home. And a man who still loves you very much."

"This is crazy," I say, and a small laugh manages to escape, but it's not the kind that means anything is funny.

"Maybe," Josie tells me, and then she turns to go. "But you should see for yourself."

I watch her leave. I watch as she closes the door behind her, and I know she's right. It's time to go home. This I have to see for myself.

I SNEAK INTO OUR BACK YARD. I CAN'T HELP MYSELF. I PROMISE myself all the way there that I just need a peek, and then I'll go. But as I watch you through the window, I'm mesmerized. You're holding the baby, and something in me shifts ever so slightly. You're cradling her, rocking her back and forth, and I swear I've never felt a lump in my throat grow this big. I wonder if it will stop growing? I wonder how much I can take, and then the tears come. But I'm not sad. I'm something else.

Before tonight, I didn't think I could ever go back in that house, but seeing the two of you now, it's all I can do not to rush in. I stand here, and I know that I should go. I know I should probably run and not look back—save myself—and yet, I can't turn away. I can't stop watching. It doesn't help your case that the stupid dog is barking, going crazy, demanding to be let out, but you keep him in. You disappear for a second from view, and I know you. You kennel him. I wonder if you know it's me out here. I promise myself I'll give it just a few more minutes, but the minutes pass, and I'm still standing in the same place. I could so easily go in. But there's the part of me who knows better. I'm not sure I can be what you want me to be.

Nevertheless, it feels odd standing on the outside looking in at what should be my life, and I wonder why you sent Josie, but now I understand. You're luring me back in, but you want it to be my choice. You have your own way of doing things, your own way of reeling me in, you always have.

But a baby, Jude?

Well, I have to say, this time, you've outdone yourself.

I GO FOR COFFEE IN THAT LITTLE PLACE WE USED TO VISIT, back when we were just dating, before we fell apart. The sun is shining, and flowers are in bloom, and it's finally starting to feel like spring. The weather and the baby and the lengths you go to make me happy change everything, and if you play your cards right, I just might go home with you after our therapy appointment.

I arrive before you, and I watch you go in. You didn't

bring the baby with you, and I wonder where she is. With Josie, I'm guessing. You look tired, weary even, and this isn't the 'you' I know. Maybe you're different. Maybe you're the same. Maybe we can make it work. Maybe we can't.

But there's only one way of knowing, isn't there?

I SETTLE IN. READY TO SEE. HOPING AND NOT HOPING, AND not knowing what exactly I'm hoping for. That's the scariest part. The wanting and the not wanting, and shouldn't it be one way or the other? Maybe love isn't definitive. Maybe it's just a choice. Go right or go left, but don't stand in the middle.

"So, tell me," the therapist says clapping his hands and interrupting my thoughts. "Who did their homework?"

You eye him with contempt, and then you look at me. You raise your brow while I offer a slight smile. I lean over and pull a notebook from my bag. You have a folder in your hands.

"First, before we begin..." he starts. "I want to hear how things have been going since our last visit?"

"Great," you say. You perk up when you say it, and I can tell you mean it.

"Fine," I tell him.

"Is there anything you want to say to each other?"

"I wrote Jude a note. I'd like him to read it... before we get started," I say, and I pass you the note.

You read it, although not aloud, and I am thankful. Then you look over at me, and I know well the expression you wear. I see a hint of a smile and something more.

Dr. C looks from me to you and then back at me. "Tell me about the letter, Kate."

I cross my legs and crack my knuckles. "It says I want to know about Amy."

He looks at you and waits.

You look at me. "I killed her," you say, and you sigh, but you don't look away.

I cock my head. "How?"

You look at Dr. C. His mouth partially hangs open. It looks as though he were speaking in mid-sentence.

"Does it matter?"

"Yes," I tell you. It absolutely matters.

"Why?"

I shrug. "It makes you different."

You frown. "How so?"

"I've never killed someone I loved."

"You would if you had to."

"Hold on a sec," the therapist says. "Are you suggesting... I'm not sure I'm following—"

I exhale, and then I roll my eyes. This guy. He's not very quick on the uptake. "Aren't you, though?" I interrupt, and confusion plays across his face.

"Why did you want these stories?" I demand as I hold my notebook up for him to see. I wave it in the air for effect.

"I told you. I find that it's cathartic for my clients to write about what they're feeling."

"Profitable too," I add.

He squints. "Excuse me?"

"Just a second... I'll get back to that," I say, and I shift in my seat to face you.

"Jude, I have to know how you killed her?"

This time, you answer definitively, and maybe it's a sign. "I drowned her."

"Where?"

"Under the bridge."

"Which bridge?"

"The one in the photo..."

"Hmmm," I say. "But there's no water here..." I say, and I realize I'm not making any sense, at least to the therapist, but that will come, and so I clear my throat and survey the room. I stand and walk to the doorway. Then I turn and ready you both for the money shot. "Why did you kill her?"

"She was blackmailing me."

The therapist starts to stand, but I hold up a finger. "Stay," I order, and you shift in your chair, ready to make him if you have to. He gets the message, and he settles back in.

"Why did you lie to me?"

You both start to speak. I stand and make my way around the room surveying the accolades that line the walls. The room goes eerily silent.

"Jude," I say again.

"It's hard to talk about...." You admit.

"Come on. *Seriously?*" I say, and you're not fooling me. "You didn't think I could handle it, did you? You didn't think I'd stay..."

You shake your head slightly. "I thought you'd always wonder."

"But I wondered anyway. I wondered if you still loved her, and I wondered what would happen if she ever showed up. I wondered how much of a hold she had on your heart, and you let me. The whole time, you lied. And for the life of me, I can't figure out which was worse in the end. The truth or the lie."

Dr. C stands and holds out his hands. "This is crazy talk... listen... I'm afraid this, this is out of my scope of expertise."

"What? Blackmail? Lying? No, I'm afraid those are *exactly* your areas of expertise," I tell him, and I shake my head. "Don't you know about Yelp? Did you not think your clients would start to talk?" I ask, and he looks away. But it isn't really a question, and I don't allow him to answer. "Of course, they would, in the only way they knew how. By writing anonymous comments online."

I clear my throat. "You are a coward in the worst way. You lie. You tell people you want to help them, and then you take their stories, their pain, and you make a mockery of it. I know it, and my husband knows it." I sigh, and then I smile. "You see, Doc, you were a peace offering. I get that now."

He stares at me, and I don't think he's ever known crazy like this. I drive the point home.

"You were a test—to see how smart I was," I chuckle. "And my husband—boy, does he ever like tests. He's a good liar, too. Like you, he's good at using people for his own personal agendas. Just ask him about that time down in Mexico he convinced me that I killed his client's daughter," I add, and I look at you. I have your full attention. "I know you just wanted to see if I would do it. I don't think you even cared either way. But you sure as hell wanted to use it to your advantage. You wanted me to think I was a liability. And the sad part is... it worked for a little while. Until it didn't."

"Kate—" you say.

"Don't Kate me. Fuck you." I take the therapist's letter opener and point it in his direction. "This is my turn to talk. That's what we're paying for, isn't it?"

"Yes," he says. His eyes give him away. He's terrified, and he should be. You should be too because I've had it with your bullshit, and someone is going to have to pay for it.

"Wrong," I say to Dr. C. "I'm not paying you to talk. I'm paying you to screw me. I know what you are. You're not so different than we are, really. You bribe your clients for money, threatening their livelihoods, their families, their reputations. They trust you, and you take them for all they've got. But the thing is, Doc—eventually, word gets out, and someone has to be held accountable. And quite honestly, this time, you met the wrong client. I'm just thankful for my husband here. He saw you for what you were, and he left it for me like a gift, all neat and packaged, just waiting to be found. Jude knows how much I like justice. He's a fan, too."

The therapist doesn't speak. He comes around and sits down at his desk. He hangs his head, and he weeps. Maybe he knows what's coming. Maybe he thinks I have a heart. I don't. Not for milking peoples' pain to make a buck. I take my Glock from the holster, which is attached to my thigh, and you raise your brow. I cock it for good measure. Then I press it to his back. He flinches. His sobs grow louder. You smile.

"Stand up and walk with me," I tell him, and I expect that he isn't going to budge, but he surprises me when he does, and I like it when that happens. As he stands, I stab the needle in his neck, I administer a little something to take the edge off, not much, and he fights then, but I'm prepared. You stand, ready to come to my aid, but the fight doesn't last long. I push the gun in harder. I tell him I'll pull the trigger and I will. It's his choice. He chooses wrong, but then in his case there wasn't a right choice, was there? Eventually, he follows us out to the empty lot.

"Where's your car?" I ask.

You look at me funny. "I took a cab."

I glare at you sideways. "Why?"

"I had a hunch," you tell me, and I wait for you to say something more, but you don't. Meanwhile, our hostage is fading fast.

I roll my eyes and dig for my keys. You open the door before I can find them, and clearly, I haven't thought this through. You motion for him to get in. He climbs in the backseat, and I scoot in beside him. You hand me cuffs, and I gesture for him to hold his hands out, and that's when the weeping starts again. I point the gun at his stomach. I don't want to get blood in my car, but I will. I'm not in a patient mood. Not with things between you and I being so unsettled.

"Please," he pleads, and I smile.

You take the driver's seat. Some things never change. "Where to?"

"The barn," I say. You look at me in the rearview mirror, and you wait. I cock my head. "You know the place. It's the one you've been following me to..."

I watch as your expression changes, and I'll never understand why you underestimate me.

"Why don't you just kill them there?" you ask.

"I like catching them off guard. Plus, it helps not having so many bodies in one spot. I don't like digging holes that much."

"It also means more crime scenes, which raises your odds of getting caught."

"Whatever," I say. You're making me look incompetent, and you're digging yourself a hole in the process.

"You could burn them..."

"Burning flesh stinks."

"So does getting caught."

You are relentless, and we argue the whole way there, back and forth, like a tennis match, and I still can't get a straight answer out of you about why you lied, about the girl in Mexico and about Amy. Maybe I never will. The therapist attempts to run interference, and I swear it's like a fucking comedy show. I guess he thinks if he fixes us, he will save himself, but then he doesn't know what you know. I've never been that forgiving.

"People lie when they're afraid," the doc offers, and he slurs his words. "Relationships can't be built on a foundation like that."

You purse your lips. "Guess you realized that a bit too

late, though, huh?" you say to him as you meet my gaze once again.

"That's ok," I assure him. "This relationship isn't built on lies. It's built on murder. We're only together because we're good at keeping each other's secrets."

He starts weeping again.

"How are you going to kill him?" you ask, but you're a smartass, and you whisper as though he isn't sitting there listening.

"I'm not," I tell you. "I'm just going to put him in the ground."

"You're going to bury him alive?" you ask, even though you know that's exactly what I plan to do.

"Yep," I say, and I laugh. "Get it? It's a metaphor."

The therapist starts to fight as the realization sinks in that this isn't going to end well. But I'm not in the mood for another fight so I inject him again using the same syringe. I give a higher dosage than I need to. But it doesn't matter if it kills him, not really. He knew what was coming.

That's what matters.

You help me put him in the ground, and then you cover him with dirt while I sit in the car. I like the AC. It's your fault we ended up seeing this shrink in the first place, and so I figure it's the least you can do to clean up the mess.

Eventually, you join me. "When did you dig the hole?" you ask, sweat dripping from your brow.

"Last week," I tell you. "It was a rough one."

You raise your brow and wipe the sweat with the back of your hand.

"I'm sorry, Kate," you say, looking out the windshield. You let out a long sigh and then you look directly at me. "I made a lot of mistakes—I'll be the first to admit that. But I don't want to end this… I don't want to throw what we have away. I love you, and I'm sorry I lied."

"What's her name?"

You think for a minute, and you do your best to read me. "The baby?"

I give you a look that says, of course, I'm talking about the baby.

You smile. "I started calling her Olive. Because she has these eyes…" you say, and your faces lights up. "They remind me of Olives. But, mostly, I've been calling her Liv. It's not permanent… but it means peace."

"Hmmm," I say.

"Really, though, I thought we could choose together."

"I don't know where to start," I tell you.

"Just say you'll come home," you plead. "We can start there."

"There's some cleaning up to do. Back at the office."

"Yes," you agree.

I check the time. "How about we start there?"

You dust your hands off on your pants.

"How long do you figure until he wakes up?" you ask.

I shrug. "Who cares?"

"Well, you should, for one."

"Why?"

"Because your hole… isn't deep enough. He could dig his way out —if he somehow manages to avoid suffocating on dirt. It's not absolute."

I bite my lip. "Sure it is," I tell you even though I'm not sure. "Is anything absolute?"

"A few things…" you say.

"Like what?"

"Love," you sigh and then you grin. "And death. Especially death where murder is involved. The odds of getting caught tend to go down," you say, and you laugh. You watch me squirm. "No worries, though," you tell me when you've had your fill. "I've got you covered."

I frown, and I realize as long as I'm with you, I'll never be bored.

"I put a bullet in his head. For good measure," you tell me, and you smile.

"Thanks," I say even though the word tastes bitter, and I don't really mean it. He probably would have choked on dirt if the drugs didn't do the trick first.

"We don't need a therapist, Kate. And we sure as hell don't need a divorce," you tell me. "What we need is each other."

"You're probably right," I say, and it's as good a concession as I can offer.

You smile, reach for my hand, and put the car in gear.

"RUDY ISN'T YOUR REAL FATHER," I SAY ON THE WAY HOME, after we've cleaned the office, after we've wiped any evidence of us having been there.

You aren't expecting me to say it, but I can't help myself.

"I know," you tell me.

"What? Really? For how long?"

"For longer than he would have liked."

"Why didn't you tell me?" I ask. Suddenly, I feel lost. You aren't fazed. "Did you know I knew?"

"I suspected."

"Did Rudy tell you that I knew?

"No. Rudy doesn't know I know. Not really, anyway."

"What do you mean?"

You let out a long sigh and then you finally look over at me. "There are two kinds of people, Kate," you say, and you pause. "Those who lie outright. And those who avoid the truth."

"So you don't believe in being honest?" Clearly, you don't. It's a pointless question. I realize this the second it slips out.

"I believe that not everything needs to be said."

As long as I live, I'll never forget what it was like, holding my daughter for the first time. I fully prepared myself not to fall in love. I was prepared to feel remorse, maybe even indifference toward her, given that she is a stand-in for what could have been. But she's more than that. And I know this the moment those olive eyes meet mine. She's just a baby who wants to be loved, and in the end, I can't help it. I might be crazy, I might be a killer, but I'm also a woman— now a mother—learning how to give the love she needs. It comes slowly at first, hesitantly, before the adoption is finalized, that is. I know what it's like to have everything swept out from under you, to have everything you love wiped out in an instant, and I won't let it happen again. We'll run if we have to. You agree that we will. Thankfully, we don't have to. Her mother doesn't put up a fight. She signs the papers, collects her money, and that is that.

We name her Olivia, but you won't stop calling her Olive. You swear you're just mocking people who give their children ridiculous names, but I think you do it to annoy me.

There was a small search for the missing therapist, but it died down just as fast as it came on. People don't miss men like that for long. Not surprisingly, few people missed him at all, and this is what makes my job so easy.

SUMMER ARRIVES, AND WE THROW A BARBECUE IN OUR backyard to celebrate our first anniversary. It's also sort of a dig at Anne, for being such a cunt about the whole charity thing, but she seems to take it in stride. When I was in the hospital, she came to apologize. Then, she sent a baby gift for Olivia, and when I decided to move back in, in order to keep the peace, I told her not to worry—that it's all water under the bridge.

I'm learning too. I could just kill her. I know this. But for now, making peace seems easier, and if nothing else, it means I have friends again, and mostly, this is why I concede. Also, I'm tired. It turns out babies help with that. They soften you, if just a little. I find it interesting and powerful the way motherhood connects women, but it tears them apart, too. For now, we seem to have found a middle ground, our little group, and I'm not sure what more I could ask for—other than them knowing the truth.

But they can't. And they won't. I'll make sure of that. Always.

Speaking of which, I continue my little side projects, although the baby has forced me to slow down a little. But when I'm in a bind, I can always count on you to help. You and I, we seem to have found our middle ground too. As a side note, those marriage books were a waste of money. And they were wrong. Babies can save marriages. We are proof.

AFTER THE BARBECUE, WE SIT IN THE KITCHEN. I STUDY THE baby monitor. You clean up.

"She's wiggling," I tell you. "But I think she'll conk out soon."

You hand me a glass of wine. "Happy anniversary," you say, and you pull a box from your back pocket. "I got you something…"

It's Tiffany. A necklace. "You didn't have to buy me a necklace," I tell you. "You bought me a baby."

You laugh. "Only the best for you."

"I got you something too," I say, smiling. You watch my face as I open the drawer. I pull out an envelope and hand it to you.

I watch as you open it carefully and pull out the picture. You examine it, and then you look up at me, confused.

"I'm pregnant," I say, and I stand up. I feel my face growing hot.

"Obviously," you say staring at the sonogram. "Wow."

"Eleven weeks tomorrow. I guess sometimes doctors are wrong."

Your face lights up, and you come around the island, and you take me in your arms. "Maybe, but I think we're just overachievers," you say, and then you pull me in and squeeze me tight.

I squeeze you back, and I don't let go. If I didn't have to, I might never. If I could, I'd stay right here in this moment forever. This is our summer. We are happy here. Fall will come as fall does, and everyone knows winter is inevitable. But for now, we're here, and there's this.

You know my secrets, and I know yours. I also know that you're capable of killing someone you love, and this makes you different. I've never killed anyone I loved, and only time will tell if I will be like you—or if I will be different.

All I know now is that I have a baby to protect and another on the way. And I know that I love you. Also, that I keep you close not just because I have to—but because I want to—and I think it's the best kind of combination a girl like me can ask for. Maybe it's the best combination anyone can ask for. Who knows.

As for us, we are lucky to have found each other, to be bound together by the blood on our hands, by our sins. Most people would say that fear is bad—in general and in marriage. But we are not most people. Fear keeps us on our toes. The blood on our hands binds us together. And there's so much work left to do. So much justice left to seek. We have big plans. Plans we discuss often. But there's time for that.

For now, here in this kitchen, I have everything I've ever wanted, and I am drunk on hope—hope we can keep it this way—hope that we can stay on the same page. Because if we can't, then that makes you right, and you know how much I hate to be wrong. It was the truth you told when you said divorce is not an option—that one of us has to die. It isn't an option. Not now and certainly, not with kids. They're game-changers.

Coming together and falling apart changed everything for me. You can't know how much you have to lose until you lose everything. I realize this now, and if we can't be on the better side of fifty-fifty odds, then we're dead in the water, Jude. We are.

~

AFTERWORD

Dear Reader,

I hope you enjoyed reading my novel. Your engagement with my work means a great deal to me.

If it was your cup of tea, I'd be grateful if you'd consider leaving a review on Amazon.

Want to be the first to know when my next book is out? Sign up for my newsletter and never miss a release. (https://britneyking.com/newsletter/)

Thank you for your support—it truly means a lot to me.

And now, enjoy a sneak peek of another one of my books…

Britney King
Austin, Texas
November 2024

ABOUT THE AUTHOR

Britney King lives in Texas with her family, two literary dogs, one ridiculous cat, and a partridge in a pear tree.

When she's not wrangling the things mentioned above, she writes psychological, domestic, and romantic thrillers.

You can find Britney online here:

Web: https://britneyking.com
Facebook: https://www.facebook.com/BritneyKingAuthor
TikTok: https://www.tiktok.com/@britneyking_
Instagram: https://www.instagram.com/britneyking_/
BookBub: https://www.bookbub.com/authors/britney-king
Goodreads: https://bit.ly/BritneyKingGoodreads
Newsletter: https://britneyking.com/newsletter/

Want to make sure you never miss a release? Sign up for Britney's newsletter: https://britneyking.com/newsletter/

ACKNOWLEDGMENTS

Many thanks to my family and friends for your support in my creative endeavors.

To the beta team, ARC team, and the bloggers, thank you for making this gig so much fun.

Last, but not least, thank you for reading my work. Thanks for making this dream of mine come true.

I appreciate you.

ALSO BY BRITNEY KING

<u>Standalone Novels</u>

<u>No Good Deed</u>

<u>I Said Run</u>

<u>Blood, Sweat, and Desire</u>

<u>The Sickness</u>

<u>Ringman</u>

<u>Good and Gone</u>

<u>Mail Order Bride</u>

<u>Fever Dream</u>

<u>The Secretary</u>

<u>Passerby</u>

<u>Kill Me Tomorrow</u>

<u>Savage Row</u>

<u>The Book Doctor</u>

<u>Room 553</u>

<u>HER</u>

<u>Around The Bend</u>

Series

The Killer Series

Kill, Sleep, Repeat

Kill, Sleep, Repeat Volume II

The New Hope Series

The Social Affair / Book One

The Replacement Wife / Book Two

Speak of the Devil / Book Three

The New Hope Series Box Set

The Water Series

Water Under The Bridge / Book One

Dead In The Water / Book Two

Come Hell or High Water / Book Three

The Water Series Box Set

The Bedrock Series

Bedrock / Book One

Breaking Bedrock / Book Two

Beyond Bedrock / Book Three

The Bedrock Series Box Set

The With You Series

Somewhere With You / Book One

Anywhere With You / Book Two

The With You Series Box Set

SNEAK PEEK: DEAD IN THE WATER

BOOK TWO

He's a contract killer. She likes to even the score. Smack dab in the middle of suburbia, few married couples are as competitive as Jude and Kate.

But then, most married couples don't keep score in the form of body counts. Each hell-bent on a silent pact to out-do the other, the games begin.

Who ends up on top is anyone's guess. But with these two, one thing's for sure— not everyone comes out alive.

After all, there are a few things they can agree on: All is fair in love and war. And if they can't make it work— they're dead in the water.

DEAD IN THE WATER

BRITNEY KING

COPYRIGHT

Hot Banana Press

Cover Design by Britney King LLC

Cover Image by Christopher Campbell |chrisjoelcampbell.com

Copy Editing by Librum Artis Editorial Services

First Edition: 2017

ISBN: 978-0-9966497-8-0 (Paperback)

ISBN: 978-0-9966497-3-5 (All E-Books)

britneyking.com

For you.
They're always for you.

PREFACE

There's a girl not long dead who rests down by
the water's edge.
Her final words were, " Please. I won't tell—I —."
She never did get the second half
of her sentiment out.
I made sure she never will.
Some things are best left unsaid, I think.
In the end, it didn't matter anyhow.
I knew she wouldn't tell.
And she knew it too.

∽

There's a girl who rests down by
the water's edge.
She was young, but you
and the water washed it all away.
Sometimes I don't get why you
do the things you do.
But you like it that way— and in a sense, I do too.

∽

CHAPTER ONE

JUDE

AFTER

Do I love my wife? Of all the questions there are to ask —*this* is what the woman sitting across from me wants to know. It's a simple question, really. Which should make the answer simple. But then, the truth is far from simple, and in our case, particularly lately, the answer's not even close to black and white.

It wasn't always this way. But you know that.

I don't answer—at least, not right away. It isn't her eyes I watch as she frames the next question, it's her lips. They linger, moving slowly as she speaks, and it doesn't help matters any that they're painted a striking shade of red. This color is a stretch for a so-called professional, and then, of course, there's the other issue—the fact that her top is unbuttoned two buttons below what I'd consider appropriate. Still, I pretend not to notice. But that's not to say it doesn't take effort. Pretending isn't all it's cracked up to be. You know that too.

This woman, whom I'm not answering, she sits legs crossed, head cocked, and she studies me. I study her too. Because what else can you do when you're avoiding things? We're in a stand-off the two of us, and I'm familiar with this territory. It led me here. It helps that I find her interesting, from the smart blonde bob that frames her face, to her long, thin legs. I try to avert my eyes, and I do my best not to stare, although that is exactly what I'm supposed to do. It's my job to make eye contact—it's what she wants, it's the other reason I'm here. And in any case, I'm married, not blind, and I won't lie, she's attractive for a woman trying to get in my head.

This kind of woman is the worst kind. We've just met and already she's trying to dissect me, as though I'm some sort of specimen, and she seems to sense that I see her for what she is. I've known more than a few like her in my time. I can see what she's thinking as she sizes me up, peering up at me as though I'm some sort of alien. It doesn't matter that I'm silent. No matter what I say, to her it'll be as though I'm speaking a foreign language, and according to her expression, she's already decided that it's one no one has understood, ever. Whatever the case, I can also see that she's equal parts put off and intrigued. I'm wondering if now would be the time to tell her I already have one just like her at home, and I sure as hell didn't come here looking for another. But, then, probably not. Every man knows that some things are better left unsaid.

"Do you love your wife?" she repeats again, and it's amusing. I know I could lie. It would be so easy just to tell her yes, I do; it would be nice to keep it short and sweet. But I can't make myself say the word. Three letters could save me. And yet, I can't make myself spit them out.

You could. But you can do a lot of things. You can reduce a man to nothing. You've always had that effect on me. It's what landed me here, in this office, in this position.

Still, it's far from over. You can knock me down, Kate. But don't be surprised when I get back up. I'm not a quitter. You should know that. Maybe you've forgotten. But you'll see.

She sighs, and she's contemplating her next move. I can see the wheels turning behind her eyes. I look away. She isn't good at hiding her feelings, and maybe she's not like you. I shift in my seat, and suddenly my throat is dry, and I realize I'm still staring at her mouth. Also, I'm in trouble. It's just, well, I've forgotten how much you can miss a person's mouth. I'd forgotten how much I could miss yours. It's coming back to me, now, here, at the most inopportune time, and suddenly I'm trying to recall the last time we kissed. I can't remember. These days, we do other things. But not that.

She clears her throat, and I glance up and meet her gaze. I wonder if she knows what I'm thinking. I think she does. My dick gets hard at the thought of kissing you, at the thought of the way it used to be. She smiles because she thinks it's about her.

Women like her always do.

How hard a question is it, Mr. —" she starts. She pauses and looks down at her tablet. "Mr. Riley?" she finishes, and she meets my eye again. She's toying with me. She hasn't forgotten my name. This woman is smarter than that. I'd be stupid to think otherwise. Luckily, I'm experienced, not stupid, and this is a game I know well. Cheryl Edwards-Steinbeck, I study the letters on her nameplate and instantly my dick goes soft. Of course, she's one of those women. You know, the kind who can't settle on just one name. Such a thing would be incomprehensible for a woman like Mrs. Edwards-Steinbeck. Please, she'd say if her guard were down, one name is for plain folk, peasants—not a woman such as herself, one with stature. She has a reputation to uphold. She wants people to know she's married—respectable— while at the same time neatly stating that she's not dependent on a man, and she's keeping her last name to prove it. It's too bad for her that I know her husband, and he says otherwise.

She folds her lips and shifts just slightly. She's displeased with silence. But then, so are you. Maybe all women *are* the same.

I want to tell her how displeased I am that I'm here, now that I've come. I want to let her know how cliché it is that she wants me to think— hell, that she wants everyone to think— she's unique, an island all her own, when she isn't. But it gets worse. Now she's trying to portray a level of incompetence in order to get me to let my guard down. Women: give them time, and they'll show their true colors. One way or another, every single time. Despite my silence, I want to tell her this, too. But I won't. Because this particular woman, I'm required to see, and she and I, we're working on a points system. Which means in order to get what I want, I can't tell her what I really think. It means I have to tread carefully, and believe me, it's a minefield.

But it's not as though I have much choice in the matter. Now that I'm in this position, now that I'm going to need to be around more, it seems I have no choice but to give her what she wants. She's my ticket in. I sort of need this job with the firm. Even though I really don't. Although nothing is as it seems, though, is it? Like Edwards-Steinbeck here, people can call themselves whatever they want and it won't change the fact that a spade is still a spade. This particular spade, I might add, has done a very good job of luring me in. Which is in part why I'm avoiding and evading. That's a skill, too. But then you know a thing or two about that. I just hope she recognizes this as a skill. I hope she sees how I am at holding out— almost as good as you.

But not quite.

This probing that's she's doing, it isn't unusual; I don't blame her. It's her job. But that doesn't mean I have to like it. Unfortunately, it's par for the course in this line of work, psych-evaluations. Which is why, for now, I play their game. They want to know I've got it together. They need to know I can maintain control at all costs. Lucky for them, I am the epitome of control. But given that, right out of the gate, we're talking about you, not me, I realize that revealing much of anything in the way of the truth won't exactly play out in my favor. Not here. Not with her.

But this lady—she is relentless. So relentless, in fact, that part of me wants to warn her about the last shrink I spent time with.

Of course, I *could* just give her what she wants. As you well know— that much would be easy. In a sense, it wouldn't be hard to tell the truth, that yes, of course, I love you. I've watched you carry and give birth to our child. I've watched you love the one you didn't carry, more than life itself. But there's also a lot I don't know how to tell this woman. Things I can't tell anyone, especially not you.

THE THERAPIST'S PHONE RINGS, INTERRUPTING MY THOUGHTS. She doesn't stand to leave or ask me to excuse her; she simply holds up her index finger and takes the call. She isn't polite, and this irritates me more than I want to let on. As she chatters away, she glances my way every once in awhile, just to ensure she has my attention. She wants to know I'm listening; she likes to wield her power, this one. But clearly she knows nothing about manners, HIPPA, or privacy in general, and so she rattles on. I wonder how much her husband tells her. Are they testing me? Trying to see if I'll reveal too much? Surely, she knows what I am. Does she care?

As I study her features, I consider how much to give when she stops being rude and starts in once more with the questions. Maybe I'll tell her everything. Maybe it doesn't matter anyway.

For now, attention is what she wants, and attention is what she gets. Her nose is narrow; her chin wide, her makeup painted on and I decide that she is at least a decade older than she's trying to let on. For one, her pencil skirt is a tad too tight, and more than a tad too short. She wears it proudly though, and to that I say what the hell. If you've got it, you might as well flaunt it. Except she's in a position where she needs to be in control, and dressing like a high-dollar hooker makes her seem less so. But then, that's her problem. My gain. When she's satisfied that she has my full attention, she ends the call.

"Tell me about your relationships, Jude," she says, and I haven't given her permission to use my first name. We aren't friends here— this is business— but then women like her aren't the kind to ask for permission. I eyeball the rock on her finger, and I offer my slyest smile. She waits patiently for an answer.

"Tell me about yours, Cheryl," I say, and her eyes follow mine to her left hand. She's mildly amused. But she hides it well. It could be the three coats of makeup, though; it's hard to tell.

She laughs, and I know my assessment was right. She's bored—with life, with work, in general and she wants to play. "That's a story for another day, Mr. Riley," she chides and suddenly she's back to formalities. Despite her inherent sense of desperation—she can read people; I'll give her that.

She glances down at her tablet again. "I see here that your wife filed for divorce several years back," she says and this one, she's ruthless. Although, I have to admit, I do appreciate the way she chooses her words carefully. These things can be life-saving.

"Really," I tell her. It isn't a question, but more of a statement. It's a word that means nothing, and yet it saves lives in this moment. It buys us both time.

"Really," she answers and then she deadpans. I watch as she glances back at her tablet, and I can tell that I make her nervous and unsure, even if she's not willing to show it. "Although… it was never completed," she adds, looking up at me. She raises her brow. "The case was withdrawn from the courts… can you tell me about that?"

"I'd rather not."

"And why is that?"

I try honesty on for size. "It's painful."

She frowns and it's obvious she doesn't buy my answer, which is really too bad. Finally, she exhales. "Ah, but Jude—you see, that's what we're here for. It's important to get to the bottom of things."

"Couldn't we give waterboarding a try instead?"

She laughs, but only a little. Then she lowers her gaze and then her voice. "In that case," she says. "I think it's time you bring her in."

I don't laugh. I don't say anything. I don't know what I was expecting her to say.

But it certainly wasn't that.

READ MORE HERE: https://books2read.com/deadinthewater

www.ingramcontent.com/pod-product-compliance
Lightning Source LLC
Chambersburg PA
CBHW051241250626
47155CB00009B/3112